FOREVER YOUNG
Featuring the CHICAGO BEARS

By
Mike DiMauro
With Christopher Michael Schildt

PublishAmerica
Baltimore

First printing

ISBN: 1-4137-1107-3
PUBLISHED BY PUBLISHAMERICA, LLLP
www.publishamerica.com
Baltimore

Printed in the United States of America

ACKNOWLEDGEMENTS

My deepest appreciation to those people who offered information, support and assistance during the writing of this book, my agent, Ron Laitsch of Authentic Creations Literary Agency; Debora F. Schildt, Christopher Schildt Jr. and Daniel Schildt. Patrick Doherty, M.D. and First Selectman Paul Eccard, Town of Waterford. The Chicago Bears: Scott Hagel, (Director of Publicity), Russ Riederer, (Physical Development Coordinator), Tony Medlin, (Equipment Manager) and Tim Bream, (Head Athletic Trainer). A very special thanks to Mr. R. W. McQuarters – Cornerback of the Chicago Bears defense. East Lyme: Andy Dousis (Head Coach), and coaching assistant Dwayne Maranda. The 2002 East Lyme Viking Football Team. Mr. Walter Bjorn, and the family of the late Coach Dick North. New London: At *The Day* newspaper, Mr. Gary Farrugia, (Editor and Publisher), Mr. Lance Johnson, (Managing Editor), Mr. Chuck Banning, (Sports Editor) and Mr. Rick Koster, (Arts & Entertainment). My beautiful wife, Karin, and our cat, Stella.

A VERY SPECIAL ACKNOWLEDGEMENT

During the writing of this book, an officer of Christopher Schildt's former police department, and a resident of the town of Waterford, was killed in the line of duty – Patrolman Joseph N. Sachatello, III. He leaves behind a wife, Lisa Cosentino-Sachatello, and infant son – Anthony Joseph Sachatello. May his courage and dedication never be forgotten.

Champion (cham'pe an) ***n.*** **1.** One who fights for another or for a cause; a defender – **adj.** Excelling over all others or against all odds **2.** A winner **3.** The Chicago Bears.

A WORD FROM THE AUTHOR

As the great sports columnist Bob Ryan of the *Boston Globe* once said when asked what he did for a living, he replied, "I'm an observer of the human condition." Perfect. And so, while some spend their lives in search of the true meaning of their existence, I search for column ideas. As a sports columnist for a newspaper in Connecticut, it's what I do for a living.

When Ron Laitsch, a literary agent from Atlanta, first called me about Christopher Schildt's story, I had one thought – *nonsense*. OK, it was actually, "barn-droppings," or at least the R-rated version thereof. According to the story I was given by Mr. Laitsch, Chris had fractured his spine playing defensive back for his high school football team thirty years ago. He was paralyzed, but eventually regained the use of his legs after extensive surgery. Three years later, he became a police officer, and was awarded the prestigious Connecticut State Police Medal of Bravery after the dramatic rescue of two children. Chris was badly hurt in the line of duty as an officer. He suffered a traumatic brain injury with seizures, and spent more than two years in a hospital, undergoing treatment to help him regain his cognitive functions. After Chris left the police department, he became a published author with Simon and Schuster. He also worked with the original cast of "Star Trek."

At the age of 45, Chris decided to lose the extra 40 pounds that he had been lugging and resurrect the football career the spinal injury denied him. He quit a two-pack-a-day cigarette habit, training like an athlete, pumping weights and running a couple of miles a day. Then, and get this, he went to the Chicago

Bears, to wear a football uniform again. The Bears were the only team willing to give Chris a chance. Mind you, this guy had a fractured spine, was once paralyzed and had a traumatic brain injury, according to the story. In the end, Chris found himself exactly where his story first began – at the high school playing field where he was injured. He was given a hero's welcome by his old team – the Vikings, and was presented with his football jersey. After a long and painful journey, Chris had finally found his way home – thirty years later.

Then I thought to myself, *what if this guy is telling the truth*? This would be a column and a half. So I listened to what Ron Laitsch had to say. I later met Chris in person. I reviewed some of the documentation, including photographs, letters, medical statements, and I spoke with Chris' neurosurgeon. It turns out that everything Ron Laitsch had told me was the truth. I also discovered that there was *much* more to the story. From the original column that I wrote for my paper, *The Day*, and a subsequent article about Chris'experience with the Chicago Bears, came the opportunity to write the story that you are about to read.

This book is based on Chris' life, which needs no embellishment. While some of the names have been changed, the story accurately depicts the depths of nowhere from which Chris Schildt triumphantly emerged, and the physical and emotional pain that this man has endured. Those who are paralyzed pray for the ability to walk again. Every old athlete prays for a second chance. For Christopher Schildt, those prayers were answered.

INTRODUCTION

By Christopher "Mike" Schildt

A larger-than-life George Halas portrait, made of ceramic tiles, stared down at me inside Halas Hall, the Chicago Bears' complex in Lake Forrest, when I arrived for training camp. I couldn't help but laugh. At 45, I'm old enough to remember when Halas coached the Bears, stalking the Wrigley Field sidelines on a Sunday afternoon, bigger than life, a link from the days when helmets didn't have face masks and pro football players were blue-collar ruffians.

Halas founded pro football in 1920, initiating a fee of $100 per team for membership. Originally the Bears were the Decatur Staleys, named after A.E. Staley, a starch manufacturer and sports enthusiast. Staley sold the team to Halas for $5,000, prior to the 1921 season when the Staleys moved to Chicago. In deference to baseball's Chicago Cubs, Halas renamed the team the "Bears" on January 28, 1922. He later explained his decision in his biography: "I noted football players are much bigger players than baseball players, so if baseball players are cubs, then football players must be Bears!" Halas' team reflected its coach's personality. The team came to be known as "The Monsters of the Midway" because of its composition of tough men. Dick Butkus personified the Bears' personality for my generation. Ball carriers always went down when Butkus hit them. The only suspense was determining whether they would get up afterward.

Hanging on the opposite wall from the Halas' portrait were framed photographs of Bears' Hall of Famers like Mike Ditka,

Gale Sayers, Doug Atkins, Butkus, George Blanda, Walter Payton, and Sid Luckman, to name a few of the many. In a trophy case, the gleaming Vince Lombardi Super Bowl trophy proclaimed the team's 46-10 win in Super Bowl XX. The Lombardi trophy is the object of desire for the 85 players already in camp for the Bears' May mini-camp, laying the groundwork to compete for another Lombardi trophy.

Dick Jauron walked past en route to a morning meeting. The Bears' coach held that dignified look that comes with power. There's something about a head coach's aura that always put the fear of God in me, dating back to my days as a defensive back for East Lyme High School in Connecticut.

Outside the sun was bright. A morning chill filled the air. Hulking players moved through the lobby and hallways toward their respective position meetings. I couldn't believe the size of the players and how chiseled they were, giving new meaning to "being in shape." More difficult to comprehend were the youthful faces, the guys who entertain America every Sunday looked more like kids to me. But then again, I was playing the game before most of them were born. Brian Urlacher walked into a meeting room, head shaved, standing around 6-foot-3, 250 pounds, the definitive athlete. Urlacher is the new generation's Butkus wreaking havoc on opposing offenses with his toughness, speed and attitude – a true impact player. He was the NFL Defensive Rookie of the Year in 2000 and an All-Pro in 2001, yet he too looked like the kid up the block you used to see working underneath the hood of some beat-up Chevy. It made me wonder. What if I had been able to finish my high school football? Would things have been different? Would I be looking back on a sports career like others who had played the game and quit on their own terms? What if I hadn't taken the hit that fractured my spine that once left me a paraplegic? Damn, if I had only seen that tackler coming for me! Don't get me wrong, I'm thankful for how things turned out. I am one of the fortunate ones – I'm not confined to a wheelchair. Still, I never did have the opportunity to take off my football uniform for a final time, 30 years ago, when the game told me I was through and I knew it was time to quit. Then again, few things ever go as planned. Now I have been given the opportunity to wear the uniform of a Chicago Bear even though I was once crippled. This is my story.

MIGHTY MOUSE

Christopher “Mike” Schildt

PROLOGUE

If you don't know anything else about southeastern Connecticut, you know this: There is no such thing as, "an East Lyme guy." The community of East Lyme, back in the 70s, was too vanilla to engender the kind of characters that give a town personality. Vanilla, not coincidentally, still matches the color of most of the residents of this small shoreline town, about 30 miles from the Rhode Island border.

Years ago, many East Lymers went to school in the old whaling city of New London. If you were part of the white flight, you were a New London transplant in East Lyme, ten miles west, seeking a better life for your kids. A better life was just another way of saying they had to get away from the blacks who had infiltrated their hometown. Who invited them, anyway? That's why vanilla was preferred. That's why Christopher Michael Schildt, a penniless kid from Florida, hated it so much. You were either one of them, or you were, "The Great Unwashed," even if you looked like Chris, with blonde hair, blue eyes and rosy cheeks, like a billboard for *Coppertone*.

At one time or another, everyone had once lived in New London, the region's hub, and home to what had been the only high school for miles, especially in the 50s and 60s. You were a "New London guy," and you liked a New London guy, because you were part of an unofficial fraternity. You knew that the kid over there might be a delinquent, but he was your delinquent, and so you took care of him. East Lyme had no character because the New London guys stayed on their turf. East Lyme certainly had no one like Humphrey, the quintessential New London Guy. His real name was Donald Scott. He was known as "Humphrey" after Humphrey Pennyworth of Bazooka Bubble Gum fame, because he was big, loud, and gregarious. Humphrey was an old bookie who used to rationalize parking in handicapped stalls by saying, "I'm the best handicapper in town."

No one in East Lyme would ever yell at a judge. But Humphrey did, a few years before he died, embattled in a bitter case with his ex-wife. When the judge sided with her, Humphrey called it a "railroad job" in the middle of the courtroom. He asked the judge to put the handcuffs on him in front, not the back, unloaded an impressive string of obscenities that his lawyer, Tony Basilica, still talks about today. Humphrey told his ex-wife that he wouldn't walk across the street to piss on her if she was on fire. East Lyme had no Humphreys. It had no identity, really. The best the town could offer was the high school football coach, a stand-up guy named Dick North.

High school football coaches get stereotyped like Miss Americas, if you haven't noticed. Miss Americas are thought to violently chomp their gum while opening their mouths so you can hear the symphony. They use "like" every third word. "It's just like an honor like to be here in like this awesome like pageant." They are thought to have invested more in their breasts than Yale professors did in their education.

High school football coaches, meanwhile, are thought to yell a lot, fart incessantly and wear those hideously skin-tight polyester shorts. They shout obscenities between exhaling into whistles, while challenging the manhood of their players. An insensitive person with a sinister sense of humor might like to get a bootleg tape of a football coach from the 1970s and bring it to a meeting of some gay and lesbian gathering on a college campus of today. Could you imagine the reactions to some old man with a crew yelling, "faggots," every 30 seconds or so? Of course, Dick North would never do such a thing. He was always a gentleman. East Lyme, actually, had a gem in Dick North. He was stocky, built like an offensive lineman with an intimidating crew cut and plain features. And yes, he wore those coaching shorts that didn't exactly augment a gut that indicated his wife, Dorothy, could cook like Julia Child.

Dick was somewhat out of place in East Lyme, Chris thought. He was a good man, with good values that he passed on to his players. Chris would come to love him. Dick, unlike many of his teammates and people in town, cared. It didn't matter who you were or how much money you had. Dick was there for you. There was no caste system on his football team. It was Coach North who had given Chris his nickname. Back in high school, Chris used his middle name – "Mike." Chris was on the kickoff squad one game when he knocked another player, who was nearly twice his size and weight, flat on his back. From that day forward the pint-sized kid from Florida, at 5-foot-9, 145 pounds, would be called "Mighty Mouse" by coach North.

Football was Chris' life. He certainly wasn't going to spend more time at home, especially with a drunk for a father. His dad was a retired military man. There was a lot of that in southeastern Connecticut with the U.S. Sub Base a few miles away in Groton, and the Coast Guard Academy in New London. His mother? She had six children – five too many for her taste. Meantime, there was football – the outlet.

Dick North, too, would anticipate football season as Chris would. All football people are that way. They could hibernate from the Super Bowl to the draft, hibernate again, and emerge sometime after the Fourth of July when it was time to get in shape. The rest of the year is an exercise in killing time, x-ing days off the calendar, until the real season begins in the fall. The weather is cooler, and in New England the leaves change, turning every glimpse onto the horizon into a Hallmark moment.

Summer's green field was still intact except for a patch or two of brown, on what would prove to be the end of "Mighty Mouse" Chris. The day began like all the others. The East Lyme players, one slightly whiter than the next, were lined up, side by side, in four rows that stretched from the end zone nearest to the school to the 50-yard line.

Chris was in the locker room dressing for today like he did every day. The leather shoulder pads went under the maroon and white practice jersey, with the number '72.' A maroon helmet with the white Vikings' logo, the same as the Minnesota Vikings, was tucked under his arm as he ran out to the practice field.

First came the stretches: arms extended, swinging in a circular motion. Jumping jacks were next. They were mostly half-assed because the players' shoulder pads prevented them from extending their arms over their heads. You could get away with that here, unlike gym class, where, inevitably, the former marine teaching you would demand 40 pushups if your hands didn't slap and make a clapping noise when they went above your head.

Then you did the hamstrings. Sit down, back straight, extend the right leg, while the left one remains tucked – lean over, and count to ten. Members of the jealous student body would walk by impressed that football players could count that high. Chris played in the secondary, which meant he'd go with the rest of the defensive backs for specific drills like reading the quarterback's eyes, making sure you see that ball when it's being thrown at the guy you're defending. It was important to listen to your teammates on the sidelines as they yelled, "PASS!" in case your back was turned and the ball was in the air. The quarterback, Palmer Whitney, began the play by dropping back. He had ample time to throw. Jesus, how a pass rush might have changed history.

Chris quickly realized the ball was going to be up for grabs. The receiver, Coleman Whitehouse, was running post pattern, meaning he would run straight off the line of scrimmage, and then veer a bit toward the middle of the field, to an imaginary post, where the ball should have been waiting for him. Whitney ended up throwing a floater. Another receiver, Stan Jaskiewicz, realized the ball would be up for grabs, too, and so he ran to the middle of the field, bringing another defensive back, Peterson Haynes, with him. There were four people running to one spot. Chris got there first and jumped, figuring he had the interception. So did Whitehouse, who was late getting there, and didn't want Chris to catch it. Whitehouse's helmet landed squarely in Chris' back, creating a cracking sound like the snap of a pencil. The collision of bodies, whistles tooting and coaches howling-- a normal day at practice-- came to an eerie standstill.

"What was that?" Dick North asked, running to the spot.

"It's Schildt!" Whitehouse said, voice trembling. He knew that something was wrong. Chris was laying face down on the turf. He wasn't moving.

THIRTY YEARS LATER

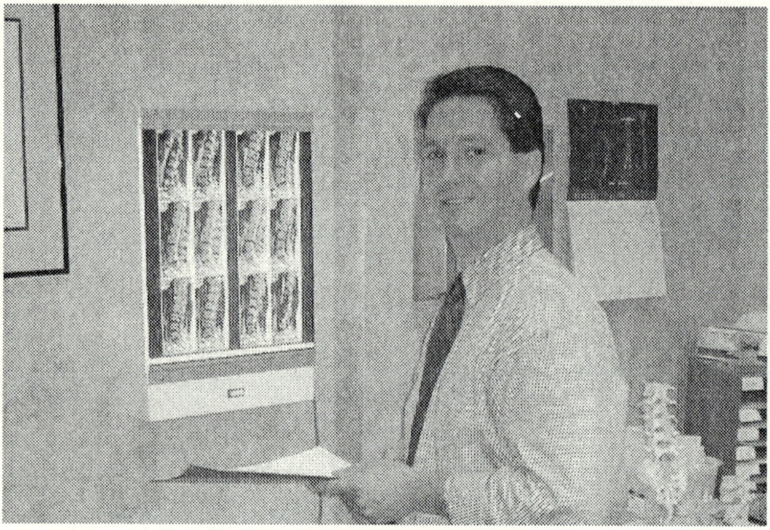

Dr. Patrick Doherty

CHAPTER ONE

October 3, 2001

"Now that's interesting," Dr. Patrick Doherty said, studying an x-ray.

Interesting? That wasn't exactly the word Chris Schildt wanted to hear from a neurosurgeon examining an x-ray of his spine, which had been hurting mercilessly.

"Interesting? Showing Dennis Franz's ass on *NYPD Blue* to somehow help the ratings-- now that's interesting," Chris said, sitting on an exam table in Doherty's office. "But my spine. . ."

Dr. Doherty turned to look over his shoulder at Chris.

He chuckled. "All right, I'll put it this way: If the people at Elias ever kept stats on x-ray histories, what I see here puts you somewhere between the Red Sox and the Cubs."

Chris, not much of a baseball fan, nonetheless knew the Red Sox and the Cubs had long, torturous existences. Still, he shrugged his shoulders.

"I still don't understand," he said.

The doctor circled an area of the x-ray showing the base of the spine with his fingertip.

"Well, we have evidence of massive trauma to the spine. These vertebras have all been fused together. Heck, they don't even look like vertebras anymore. Farther north, we can see where a couple of the ribs were broken."

Doherty's smile from before faded.

"I'm surprised you're even walking. Did this happen when you were a police officer?"

"An old football injury," Chris said. "Thirty years and about

70 pounds ago."

It was true. Chris still had blonde hair, even though his temples had turned gray. He still wore Levi's and sweatshirts, as he did when he was a teen. His facial features made him look like Phil Simms, the old Giants quarterback, except that he looked like Simms only if he had finished his career as a left tackle. Chris was a good 40 pounds overweight and smoked two packs of cigarettes a day. Walking up a short set of stairs made him huff and puff like the wolf in "Little Red Riding Hood." He wasn't very tall, only 5-foot-9, which made the extra pounds more pronounced. The speed, muscle and boyish good-looks from his youth were gone, replaced by the sight of a frail man, quickly growing old.

"Was there paralysis?" Doherty asked.

At first, Chris answered him by slowly nodding his head. Then he said, "But I don't know what was worse. The pain, not being able to move my legs, the loneliness or the pneumonia."

"Pneumonia?" Doherty said, looking at him curiously. "What about pneumonia?"

"A couple of weeks after surgery I developed pneumonia. I was moved to the Intensive Care Unit. It was *that* bad. I couldn't breathe without oxygen. My weight had dropped to 90 pounds. Once, I caught a glimpse of myself in a small mirror on a table next to my bed in I. C. U. There was only a thin layer of pale skin, and dark circles under a set of bloodshot eyes. I had become unrecognizable even to myself. My doctors were certain that I was going to die. It really was *that* bad."

Doherty cocked his head, appearing more bewildered than he was when he had studied the x-ray of Chris' spine. "What do you mean?"

"I was unconscious, most of the time," Chris said. "But one night I heard the sound of a voice whispering in my ear. It was a priest, a Catholic priest. He was giving me the 'Last Rights.' I'm a Lutheran, not Catholic. It said so in my charts. But that's how bad it was. The I. C. U. needed someone-- anyone-- fast. Apparently, they felt that they didn't have the luxury of time to summon a Lutheran. I would guess that the Catholic was the only one available. If it had been a Rabbi working the ward that night, I suppose I would have heard Hebrew being whispered into my ear. But no, it was a Catholic priest."

It was Doherty's turn to slip into a brooding silence, as he starred at Chris with an expression of sympathy.

"No, the loneliness. . . No, that was the worst," Chris added.

"What about your friends? Your teammates?" Doherty asked, timidly.

"No one," Chris replied, slowly shaking his head. "Oh, my coach, Dick North, stopped by a couple of times. He was even there on the day they did the surgery. Coach North brought me my jersey as a gift. But someone had stolen it when I was moved to the Intensive Care Unit. There were the nurses, of course, and a janitor, who cleaned the room every morning at precisely 9:15. Other than that, there was no one. There were times when a stranger simply saying hello was enough to put a smile on my face.

"The only thing worse than the loneliness was the knowledge that I would never play football again. I would never get dressed in a locker room. No more leather shoulder pads or the sound that a helmet made when a chin strap was snapped on. No more walking from the locker room to the field, helmet tucked under one arm. And even though most of my teammates wouldn't even talk to me, it was still better than sitting home alone.

"Hatred was the only thing that helped to pull me through there in that hospital. I hated the town of East Lyme, especially the kids I went to school with. I hated God for not even showing enough mercy to allow me to die a peaceful death. But of all the people and things that I hated the most was my own mother and father, who had put me in that agonizing situation to begin with, and who never even bothered to come and visit me or to be there on the night that I was given my 'Last Rights.' A dog was treated better than I was, back then."

"What about the rest of your family?" Doherty asked, his voice closer to a whisper.

For a second time Chris slowly shook his head.

"No one!" he said. "For over six months I was alone. There wasn't even another patient to talk to. I was in a room by myself. But I was lucky to have a room in the middle of the hall near the nurse's station. I could hear their voices. I could hear the gossip, 'Did you hear about Liz and the intern? Liz might be pregnant. They did it on one of the examination tables. She yelled so loud, a patient nearby rang the nurse's button in fear of someone's safety, which is how they got caught.'"

Doherty chuckled. Then he pointed to Lawrence and Memorial Hospital, which was across the street from his office, there in New London. "This was at L&M?"

"The Groton Sub Base," Chris replied. "My father was retired military, and back in the 70s, the base had a fully functioning hospital and a surgical staff. Not like today.

"When it was time to leave the hospital I was sent to live with my brother, Jimmy, in Florida. My parents said that the warm, dry climate would be better for me. Truth was that they didn't want me. So they bought me a one-way bus ticket, handed me a $5 bill for food, and then dropped me off at the Greyhound bus station in New London. They didn't even wait with me. But that was all right. My brother Jim had always been more of a father to me than that drunk who had brought me into this world. It was Jimmy who had taught me how to throw a football. He was the one to tuck me in at night when I was small. Jimmy was blinded in Viet Nam, and had lost most of his hearing. Despite his physical handicaps, he was still a great father to me. He understood how it was with my mother and father. He was as emotionally abused by my parents as I was. A couple of years later, I became a police officer. I was later forced to retire after a head injury in the line of duty."

Chris and his partner, Rob Wilson, working the midnight shift, were running radar in the parking lot of Beit Brothers, a supermarket in Montville, on Rt. 32. The drill rarely changed: sit there with the radar gun waiting to catch someone driving too fast in either direction.

They spotted a car driving erratically. The driver had to be drunk, so they thought, and so both officers took off after him. The vehicle appeared to welcome the challenge driving on the wrong side of the road, as he increased his speed. He crossed over the town line to the city of Norwich on Route 32, and for whatever reason, drove into the parking lot of a fashionable health spa.

By then, Chris and Rob had been joined by a state trooper and two Norwich officers as they surrounded the driver, who had locked himself in the car. The suspect gunned the engine, indicating he'd think nothing of running one of the patrolmen over. Chris smashed the driver's side window, and then grabbed the keys out of the ignition. In the process, Chris' arm was torn open from the jagged glass.

When they pulled the driver from the car, a fight ensued. The suspect was a big man, and pumped for a fight that lasted for several minutes. He was punching each of the officers until they were finally able to get him on the ground. There were five officers pinning him down on his stomach. Still, he had enough strength to roll over and kick Chris in the forehead, causing him to fall backwards. Chris' head violently struck the corner of a steel bumper of one of the police cruisers. When the fight was finally over, Chris was taken to the hospital. Rob Wilson later discovered that the man had a trunk full of weapons. There was no doubt that he would have used them on the officers, if he had the chance.

Chris had a concussion and a fractured skull, something that was missed by the emergency room physician. The doctor never even ordered a simple x-ray. Instead, he sent Chris home and told him to get some rest. But it was Debbie, Chris' wife, who noticed that his symptoms were getting steadily worse. He was using bottles of aspirin a day, eating them like candy. Chris was always nauseous, even at work. Debbie couldn't understand why Chris, who was normally attentive, tuned her out, staring without so much as blinking an eye. She had no idea of the head injury's severity, instead growing frustrated with her husband, wondering why he was constantly ignoring her.

One night, Debbie looked into Chris' eyes and noticed that his pupils were visibly unequal. Combined with the headaches and constant nausea, Debbie insisted that he go see another doctor.

Again, Chris was misdiagnosed. He was told that his problems were related to stress from working as a police officer.

A month later, Chris called Debbie at work. He was standing somewhere in Rhode Island, unaware of how he got there. His mood swings would be violent, yelling at Debbie and the kids for things he wouldn't remember 30 minutes later. He would smash things in the house, and then wonder how something got broken. No one knew what the problem was. The children were confused, and sometimes Debbie would sleep in the boys' room.

There were nights when Debbie slept next to Chris, awakened by his body tremors. He shook uncontrollably in his sleep, making Debbie think that he was about to fall out of bed. In the morning, Chris wouldn't remember a thing.

Chris' mood swings largely went unspoken in the house. He was not aware of them, and the rest of the family was frightened by them. He had even done things at work, such as smash office furniture against a wall, and lost his temper with fellow officers. It wasn't until another trip to a doctor, a neurologist at Yale-New Haven Hospital, that Chris was finally diagnosed with a traumatic brain injury with a seizure disorder. He was immediately placed on anticonvulsants. The massive injury he had received in the line of duty was finally diagnosed properly, but by then there was little that could be done for him. The damage was too severe.

Chris spent the next two and a half years in and out of hospitals. He was a regular in the seizure units, and with a neuropsychologist at Yale, Dr. Robert Novelli. Much like the fractured spine and paralysis that ended his time on a football field, Chris'career as a police officer was finished. a career highlighted by the medal of bravery that he won after the rescue of two children with Rob from a frozen swamp in the middle of the night. What might have proven to be an enduring legacy in the field of law enforcement ended one shift in an empty parking lot. He takes countless pills to this day to control the seizures and terrible side effects of a brain injury. That is why he now spends most of his time alone.

"And the rest is, as they say, history," Chris said solemnly.

Jesus, what a tragic history, Doherty thought to himself. He cleared his throat to speak.

"Well, the spine looks great," he said. "I have no

explanation for this, except to say that you were damned lucky to have a couple of fine surgeons work on you, 30 years ago. No need to worry about surgery. In fact, I wouldn't operate, not even if you asked me to. As you said yourself, you're lugging a lot of extra weight. How much exercise do you get?"

Chris shrugged his shoulders. "I don't know. It's about 33-feet from the kitchen to my office at home where I write."

"Well, I want you to do more walking, not just to the kitchen," Doherty said, smiling. "How much do you smoke? And don't fib. I can smell it on your sweatshirt."

"About two packs a day," Chris answered.

Doherty looked at him sternly. "That's two packs too many! Let's see if we can do something to quit, and start getting some exercise. Maybe some walking, especially after meals. What about liquor? How much do you drink?"

"Not at all. Not with epilepsy."

"The seizures, are they from childhood or the head injury when you were a police officer?"

"The head injury."

"All right, I'll note that in your chart," Doherty said. Then he walked closer to Chris and put a hand on his shoulder. "What happened 30 years ago is over. None of that can hurt you anymore, unless you let it. And you are *way* too young to be slowly destroying yourself like this, between the weight and the smoking. Look, you're having back pains due to your weight. Drop the pounds, get some exercise to strengthen your muscles and you won't have some of the aches that you feel now. That's about the best I can do, especially for a guy with a broken spine."

When Chris left the doctor's office, he decided to take a stroll. It had nothing to do with Doherty's advice. Chris just didn't feel like going home. He turned up the collar to his old barn jacket, and then lit a cigarette. It was a beautiful fall day, a bit chilly with wind swept leaves of orange, red and yellow falling on the cracked sidewalk.

He limped his way down the street, where he saw a fieldstone church and an abandoned factory with broken windows. There was a row of rundown homes, much like the shabby boarding house Chris lived in when he was seventeen, until he could no longer afford the $15-a-week rent. Then he lived on the streets, sleeping in bathrooms and eating the leftover food thrown in the garbage at the local Burger King or McDonalds. That food, thoughtlessly discarded at the end of a business day, becomes the cuisine of the homeless by night. Farther up the street, Chris saw a group of children playing in an abandoned car without tires. Abandoned factories and junked cars are the playgrounds of the poor, especially for the blacks. These were the children who knew that Santa Claus came from the Salvation Army not the North Pole. Being poor was something that Chris understood all too well. He was fluent in the spoken language of the poor, of hatred, and of bigotry, especially back in Florida where he lived as a child during the 1960s.

Chris was old enough to remember the signs posted on store fronts and restaurants that read "No niggers allowed." He remembered the city buses, traveling a route from Homestead to Miami, when blacks sat in the back. That's the way it was in the South, especially with Chris' mother. She detested blacks with a passion.

His mother didn't keep her hatred to herself. To the contrary, Chris' mother was vociferous about her contempt for all ethnic groups. There was one occasion that he remembered vividly when a group of city workmen, mostly black, were working in the street in front of their home in Homestead. It was the middle of a hot summer day. One of the men walked up to the house and asked if he could get a drink of water from the outdoor faucet. Chris' mother went into the garage, got a steel rake and chased him out into the street. When she reached the edge of their property, his mother stood shaking the rake at the rest of workers, calling them, "dirty niggers," and threatened to call the police. All that the men wanted was a drink of cool water. That's the world in which Chris grew up. That was the essence of his childhood.

His mother's hatred for blacks grew worse over the years even though attitudes were starting to change.

Chris' father was more of a closet bigot. He could be polite enough with a black person when he had to. He would even say hello quite graciously. Still, Chris remembered him telling him to immediately wash after shaking the hand of a black. He told me that they were "dirty people," and to stay away from them as much as possible.

When Chris lived in Homestead, in the early 1960s, his father worked at a car dealership. The owner had served in the military with him. They were both officers. Virtually all of the car salesmen where either in the military, moonlighting now or retired. Times were different back in the early 1960s. Being a car salesman was a hot profession, turning over 30 to 40 units or car sales, in a week. The competition was fierce for those jobs. A car salesman made big money.

Suspecting that his dad was fooling around with other women, Chris' mom used to send him to the dealership as often as possible. He was there as her personal spy. Chris was there every weekend, from sunup to sundown. Truth be told, she was right, but Chris never said so. There was enough fighting in their house mostly due to the alcoholism. When Chris' father would go on of those "extra long test-drives" with a female customer, Chris would spend his time in the service department. That's where he developed his passion for cars. Chris loved to watch the mechanics at work. Back in the 1960s the mechanics were usually white. The blacks, who worked in the service department of the dealership, were only allowed to clean and prep the new cars for show or for delivery. Their crew leader, whose job it was to oversee the black staff in the service, was a man named Mr. Clayton. He was probably the finest man Chris had ever met. Mr. Clayton was a bit on the stocky side, and always wore a straw hat. He nursed a cigar butt in the corner of his lips with the sleeves to his white shirt rolled-up, revealing a pair of muscular arms. Despite his obvious physical strength, Mr. Clayton was a soft-spoken, gentle person with a sense of goodwill towards all. This was a man who hated no one.

So that's where Chris stayed most of the time back in the service department. That's where he was treated the best. Those so called "dirty niggers" were kinder and more attentive to him than his own father. The guys understood how it was with his family. African-Americans where simply not permitted to enter most of the restaurants or convenience stores. So Chris would often run errands for the guys. Otherwise, they would have no way of getting their lunch, or cigarettes, chewing tobacco or even a pack of gum. Mr. Clayton called it "the underground railroad." And Chris was only too happy to do so. Being white meant that Chris could go anywhere the men needed him to go, until the merchants found out what the boy was doing. Chris was viewed as no better than a black himself, banned from most of the businesses around the dealership. He was called "a filthy nigger lover."

It was this sort of injustice that prompted Chris to become a police officer later in life. And when he was presented with his badge, Chris thought of Mr. Clayton and the others, back in the service department, those "dirty niggers," who had loved and cared for him as a boy.

CHAPTER TWO

Chris rolled out of bed shortly after 8 a.m. Debbie had already left for work. He went to the kitchen for a cup of coffee from the pot that Debbie faithfully prepared before she left the house. Then he walked down stairs to the family room, over to the fireplace, and lit a cigarette. He always had his cigarettes by the fireplace where he could blow the smoke up the chimney when he exhaled. After a cup of coffee and three cigarettes, Chris threw on his jeans, a blue flannel shirt and a tattered, faded University of Connecticut baseball cap. He limped his way outside to his 1989 blue Jeep Wrangler, for his morning drive to clear his thoughts before writing. It was just a part of his daily ritual.

He decided to take the highway down Route 395 from the Village area of Waterford to the next town over, East Lyme. The Village is Waterford's northernmost section, bordering Montville, where Chris used to work as a police officer. Any trip to East Lyme in the morning meant a visit to Gorton Pond.

He found his favorite spot by the lake, a shady haven on Route 161 between the businesses he had just passed and downtown Niantic, two miles south. Downtown Niantic was New England quaint with storefronts that stretched alongside Long Island Sound. Chris pulled off the side of the road away from cars, and stepped out of the Jeep. The changing leaves turned the scenery into a kaleidoscope of red, orange, gold and green. The colors reflected off the crystal water of the lake. Chris didn't need to look at the trees for the foliage, just the water, especially on days like this when the water was calm. Chris looked into the water and saw the same colors and the few clouds that dotted the morning sky. New England in the fall is what heaven must look like, or should look like, Chris thought. He was about to light another cigarette when he smelled the burning wood from the chimney of a nearby house. It made him think of home, especially on a fall Sunday: The family gathered around the television watching a football game and a crackling fire burning in the fireplace. A New England Sunday in the fall: football, the family, the food and the fireplace. There was never a better time to be alive.

Farther out in the lake Chris saw what must have been a father and a son in a small boat. It looked like they were fishing or they might have simply been enjoying the scenery, like Chris. Then he saw the man pour something into a cup for the boy from a thermos. It couldn't have been coffee. The boy was too young. Cider! That's what it must have been. Hot apple cider. How appropriate for a chilly autumn day on a lake.

Cars zipped up and down Route 161 at any time of day. Chris heard nothing. It was almost as if he were home at his computer, focused on his writing. Sometimes when Chris would write, he would be oblivious to the world around him. The world, for this brief and glorious period, was about Chris, the lake, the scenery, the cider, the father and the son. After about ten minutes, Chris took one last look at the scenery, as he lit his cigarette. Then he headed for the Jeep. There was only one stop left to make before returning to his office at home to write. When he turned, he felt a lightning bolt of pain shoot up his spine. It was nothing that he hadn't felt more than a dozen times a day.

A short distance away, Chris turned into the driveway of East Lyme High School, the very same school he attended as a boy. He parked in the lot next to the football field named in honor of his former coach Dick North. The coach died in 1998, six months after the administration alerted him of changes forthcoming in the athletic department, and that his services would be no longer required. There was a lot of controversy about that in the local paper. Chris never did understand how they could have treated such a wonderful man like that. Then again, Chris wasn't treated much better.

The field had bleachers with about 20 rows stretching from one end zone to the next on the home side, not far from the Flanders Elementary School. The visitors' side had seating for roughly 200 people with only a fence separating the two square-shaped sets of bleachers from the baseball press box behind them. East Lyme's baseball field, sight of many night games and past American Legion state tournaments, sat adjacent to the football field, giving the school perhaps the region's top sports complex.

The north end zone was near the Flanders Fire House making for some interesting sounds when a fire happened during the game. Many times fans that had grown used to a football game's clamor--officials' whistles, pads smacking together, the voice of the public address announcer-- were awakened by the sound of the fire alarm. East Lymers also heard some amusing sounds beyond the outfield fence of the baseball field, quite audible in the football bleachers. A fish market that offered some outside dining wasn't far from the left field fence. Occasionally, a market worker would use the loudspeaker to alert a customer that his or her food was ready, sounds that carried an impressive distance. Football fans knew the names of the people having fish and chips for dinner. Chris sat quietly in the Jeep, watching the boys practice on the field. The days of leather shoulder pads were long gone, but the white practice jerseys remained the same, and the helmet with the logo of the Minnesota Vikings. Then he spotted number 72, his old number. He stepped out of the Jeep and limped toward the bleachers to get a closer look. Rather than standing along the fence, Chris decided to sit in the bleachers at the top row. The climb was hard on his spine, but he wanted to be close to the press box, his second home when he was kid. When he reached the top of the bleachers, Chris noticed that the press box door was open. He took a peek inside. Nothing had changed. The same nail was sticking out of the floor. It was the same nail on which he had once scratched his head, trying to get some sleep one night.

Home life was never good for Chris when he was a student at East Lyme High School, especially when his father and mother were drunk. As a small boy, Chris would hide in the closet, under a bed or just stay in his room with the door locked, when his father got real bad, which was most of the time. The press box was bigger than a closet, but not as warm.

Chris would tie his belt around a pile of clothes before leaving home, and then head to the press box, his only place of refuge. Football was his only outlet anyway, so why not the press box for a home? In the morning, before the other students arrived, he could take a shower in the locker room. Once, he tried to start a fire to stay warm. He didn't have a winter coat, so he dressed in as many layers of clothes as he could. But that was modest. So he shivered, watching his breath, as he tried to fall asleep. At least the press box was dry.

Chris walked with his head down a lot in those days. He was always looking for loose change on the floor of the school. There used to be a farmer's market in the 70s near the high school. Chris would sneak in there at night and take some fruit and vegetables, leaving change on the counter when he had it to spare. It was easy to pry the window open with his fingers and get in quickly without being noticed. The law would have called it breaking and entering, but Chris called it survival.

Wally Bjorn, a student counselor at the high school and an assistant coach under Dick North, had an idea of what life was like for Chris. He must have. Mr. Bjorn had tried hard to get Chris to come over to his house, at least for a dinner. Chris never accepted his invitations. It's not that Chris didn't trust him. To the contrary, he had come to admire Mr. Bjorn as much as Dick North. He was just too ashamed. So, it was the press box and whatever spare change he could find.

In 1971, Chris' family had moved to Connecticut. His father managed to drink up just about all the money they had, which wasn't very much. They put their house in Cocoa Beach up for sale. It was the only thing to do. Otherwise, the bank would have foreclosed on the property. His parents found a buyer fairly quick, accepting the first offer the buyer made. The good graces of the next-door neighbors, who let Chris and his parents stay at their house until his father put together enough money to move them north, prevented the family from sleeping in the car.

They arrived in Connecticut just in time to see the fall foliage, a sight that Chris had never seen in his life. The family had lived in Colorado for a time and a few other places like Iceland when his dad was in the military. But Chris had never seen anything like fall in New England, with every color imaginable. The air was crisp, unlike the sometimes oppressive heat of Florida. Even at the age of 14, Chris was enchanted with such beauty. Then it turned cold, so very cold. Still, Chris didn't mind it at all. To him, it is one of the most beautiful places on earth. Chris remembered driving down the highway, his face pressed up against the side window of the car, when they arrived in Connecticut. He saw all sorts of things that amazed him, including old cemeteries with head stones dating back to the seventeenth century. There where red barns and covered bridges, things that Chris had only seen in movies, but didn't know actually existed.

His father had found a place to rent near the beach in East Lyme, at an area called Rocky Neck. And while the scenery was beautiful and inviting, the kids at East Lyme High School were another story. Months passed, and still no one even acknowledged Chris' existence, with the exception of his guidance counselor, Mr. Bjorn. He would often pull Chris into his office for no particular reason other than to chat. He always asked him how things were going at school. And if he saw Chris in the hallway, he'd invite him to the teachers' lounge for a juice or milk. He had called Chris' parents in for a meeting, just to get a clear picture of what was going on at home. Mr. Bjorn had come to understand that Chris' home life was terrible, especially with parents who were abusive alcoholics. Chris' parents drinking only got worse. At the same time, they seemed to blame him for all of their mistakes and misfortunes. It had reached a point when Chris simply couldn't take it anymore. He had grown tired of hiding from them in his room, or in a closet, as Chris had done throughout his childhood.

So, one morning he put his clothes together in his school bag and said his goodbyes. He left the house as if he was going to school. There were some railroad tracks that ran through East Lyme. Amtrak rode the entire shoreline. Chris walked the railroad tracks that morning over to the next state, Rhode Island, where he found a Navy recruitment office. There was a kid Chris knew from Florida, who would be about 18 at the time. Chris tried to impersonate him and join the Navy, at the age of 14. Chris had hoped that the Navy would send him far away from his parents and the kids at school. The recruiter didn't fall for it. Chris never did get into the Navy. Instead, he told the boy to have a seat in a small office.

He was certain that the recruiter was going to call the police, and now, Chris would be going off of to jail. He honestly didn't care. Jail, to him, was better than going back home again, and that's what Chris told the told the recruiter.

"Call the police. Have them arrest me," Chris said tearfully. "I want to be arrested."

He didn't call the police. Instead, the recruiter told Chris that he called the Salvation Army and explained that he had a young man who was in need of assistance from an abusive home. They immediately dispatched someone to place Chris in a shelter. He stayed there for a few days, then it was back down the tracks again, to the only friend Chris had in this world, Mr. Bjorn. Chris met with him in his office after he returned to East Lyme. Running away from home wasn't the answer. Still, Mr. Bjorn knew that Chris had to get out of that house, if only for a while. Mr. Bjorn decided that Chris should become involved in a sport. So that's how Chris was introduced to football. That's when his passion for the game began. It was a decision that would change his life forever.

Chris slowly closed the door to the press box with a sense of reverence for the old place. Strange, but it was like seeing an old friend again who had cared for him when he was a boy, at a time when a place to sleep was hard to find. Then he hobbled down the bleachers and took a seat to watch the boys practice on the field, especially number 72.

The team was practicing on the sled, a gadget that replicates a lineman opposite them. Chris had been reading about his old team, the Vikings, in the paper. It was three days removed from one of the biggest wins at the school in a long time. They had beaten Norwich Free Academy, the largest school in the league, with a late touchdown. East Lyme's coach, Andy Dousis, was the first one in the pig pile after the game. The Vikings, who had been a doormat for a long time, now had a 3–0 record. The reporter at the game had printed part of Dousis' post-game speech to his team, an emotional oratory at the 50-yard-line. The players, all on one knee, with helmets tucked under their arms, hung on their coach's every word.

Nobody else but us understands what this feels like right now! Not your mother! Not your grandmother! Nobody knows how hard we've worked! Nobody knows what it feels like to be a part of this!

It nearly made Chris cry. He read the words, but thought of Dick North. He read the words, but felt himself in the mass of players on one knee, listening to his coach, like the old Viking warrior that he was.

Chris decided to move a little closer to the field. He stepped down slowly, until he reached the ground in front of the bleachers, and then limped over to the fence. Chris was close enough to hear the coaches. He caught a glimpse of Dousis. There was something about Dousis, a former Marine, that reminded Chris of Dick North. It was the short hair and his demeanor. Dick wasn't much of a screamer, mostly a teacher. Dousis and the team were about to work on their offensive strategy for the game that weekend.

The player with number 72 had gotten lost momentarily. Chris' eyes scanned the field for him. It was easier to feel like a part of the team if he could watch the kid with his old number. At the same time, Dousis had finished speaking to the team. Now it was Duane Maranda's turn. Duane, a former football player for East Lyme, was the defensive coordinator, who also worked as an East Hartford fireman. His defense had limited Norwich to seven points the previous Friday. His talk with the team wasn't about what they had done, but rather, what they needed to do for the next game.

When Chris moved a little closer he could see number 72 again in the cluster of players. He couldn't help but notice that his number-sake was in desperate need of a shave. Oh, if Dick North had seen that. Dick North had a philosophy: 'Never cultivate on your face, that which grows wild on your ass.' All things considered, this was turning out to be a pretty good day. Practice was almost over. When Duane Maranda finished speaking, a couple of players walked over to the bench close to the fence where Chris was standing. The kids needed a drink of water. No one really noticed him standing there until Chris started coughing. It was a smoker's hacking cough.

"Have another cigarette," one of the players said sarcastically. He was wearing number 40 something. Then he turned to the boy standing next to him wearing a number in the 70s. "Who's he?"

"Who cares?" another player said.

Chris cleared his throat and smiled at the boys. He gave them a timid wave.

"Fat old man!" a kid chuckled.

He said it loud enough for Chris to hear him. The group of players broke out laughing. Chris' hand slowly dropped to his side and his smile from before faded. He turned to walk away from the field back to his Jeep with the sounds of laughter following him like a shadow from behind.

Chris' son, Dan; wife, Debbie, and son, Chris

CHAPTER THREE

Debbie Schildt is exactly what a pregnant woman needs to see at an OB-GYN office where she worked as an office manager. She was a petite, 5-foot-1, blonde with blue eyes, rosy cheeks and a warm, motherly nature. Debbie looked as if she belonged in a Nestlé's chocolate commercial, handing out piping hot beverages to the men who had just come in from shoveling snow. Her demeanor and soft voice were calming as a summer breeze, giving comfort in an office where fear of the unknown and fear of the future are as real to the patients as the lives they carry within the womb.

She was just out of high school when Debbie first met Chris. It was the summer of 1978. Her friend from childhood, Carol, was dating Chris' roommate at the time. Chris was working as a police officer in Montville, a quiet, rural town just north of Waterford. Debbie walked into the apartment where Chris lived. It was one of those 'you had me at hello' situations, straight from the movie, *Jerry McGuire*. Likewise for Chris. They were married in December six months later.

Debbie usually left work shortly after five in the evening. She drove over the Gold Star Memorial Bridge, which linked Stonington, Mystic and Groton with New London and Waterford. Debbie took the Vauxhall Street Extension exit, like always, hung a right, then drove into "the Village" of Waterford. It was a part of her daily routine.

The Village is what a neighborhood should look like in a television show about family life. The loudest noise is a lawn mower. Driveways have no cracks. There are gardens that adorn the yards of beautiful New England style homes. The residents who walk the street for exercise don't have to lock their doors if they don't want to. In the Village, there is no crime.

The house where Debbie and Chris lived was located on a corner lot. It was a multi-level colonial, designed to dominate the scenery with a front yard that resembled a public park. Inside, there was a family room with a red brick fireplace. The walls were decorated with mementos from the various books Chris had written mostly having to do with Frankenstein and Dracula, including autographed pictures of the old horror movie stars, such as Boris Karloff and Bela Lugosi. The living room looked like a lobby at a plush five-star hotel with original oil paintings, illuminated by brass portrait lights. Everything was custom made, including the raised paneled walls, the hand-carved cherubs, fireplace and furniture. The oak floors throughout the second floor were covered by ornate oriental rugs. It was a showpiece, created through Debbie's imagination. There was an old English style formal dining room, with a mahogany table, chairs and hutch imported from England. A glass door offered a panoramic view of a sun room and a swimming pool with its Hawaiian style gardens.

Still, the family room was their favorite to use. It was simple. The furniture by the fireplace might have been old, but it was comfortable and the room was warm, unlike the old press box at the East Lyme playing field from years ago. It was just as cozy as the small cottage where Debbie was raised as a child in the Quaker Hill section of Waterford. The office that Chris used as a writer was connected to the family room. Its built-in bookshelves contained a wonderful assortment of antique books, mostly written by Washington Irving, and toys from the 1960s. There was even a magnificent nineteenth century edition of Charles Dickens," and Mary Shelley's "Frankenstein."

Chris often said that of all the books ever written, *Christmas Carol* and *Frankenstein* best described all that was truly wrong or right with humanity. There was a custom framed reproduction of a Houdini poster hung on a wall next to his desk. Harry Houdini, who gained fame as a great magician and escape artist, was Chris' boyhood hero. The house where he and Debbie lived was proof that Chris had become quite the magician and escape artist himself. The entrance of the house, a small lobby that divided the upstairs living room and the family room, was decorated in an African motif, reflecting Chris' travels to Egypt and Africa. The entire house seemed to make a statement: "I have stood for hundreds of years, and will stand for hundreds of years yet to come." The master bedroom was located on the third floor over the family room.

Sometimes, Chris and Debbie could hear their two sons watching television at night or laughing with their friends, before falling asleep. The room made no such sounds anymore. The boys had moved away to college, leaving behind a house that, at times, was as quiet as a graveyard. If it hadn't been for the two dogs, Max and Monster, barking when they heard a sound outside, the house would make no sound at all. Chris Jr., a rather quiet, intelligent boy, who had bright, blonde hair like his parents, was a senior at Yale. The younger of the two, the athlete, was Dan, a freshman at the Mass Maritime Academy, in Massachusetts. Dan was a very handsome kid, who looked like Prince William. The girls adored him. The boys were two very different people with very different interests. Still, they had one thing in common, the memories from their childhood. There was dinner every night at the kitchen table, talking about their day at school. There were ghost stories read by the fireplace in the fall and winter. They cooked marshmallows at the end of a stick over a fire in the backyard, and there were camp-outs in the fort that Chris built for them. It was the simpler things in life, yet most enjoyable, that had forever bonded the lives of these four very different people. There were moments of great joy, moments of great sorrow. There was Debbie's kiss on the forehead at night before mom and dad themselves settled into bed.

This is what life was like over in a small corner of the Village.

CHAPTER FOUR

NEW YORK CITY

Ron Laitsch sat down at a table by the window in a small coffee shop. The table offered a perfect view of the street outside, the Avenue of the Americas. The crowd of pedestrians racing down the sidewalk, the racket from horns blowing and engines humming, made it feel like everyone in the city was late for something. Ron chuckled. He couldn't help himself. It was a bit different than Atlanta where he worked at Authentic Creations as a literary agent. Atlanta, too, was a busy city, but the scene outside was all the illustration necessary to explain the term, New York minute.

Ron sipped on one of the flavored coffees of the day, Mocha Kenya something. The coffee shop was fairly quiet, except for a woman behind the counter taking orders. She repeated everything, perhaps to confirm what she just heard, but with a nasal voice, as if she had the flu. The smell of fresh-brewed coffee, with the wafting scent of cinnamon rolls, made the place smell more like a bakery. Ron flew into the city the night before from Atlanta. The idea was to come to New York and meet with all of his clients at once. Chris had the 10:15 a.m. slot. Ron arrived wearing his blue business suit with a white shirt and red power tie. The agent from Atlanta was a handsome man, who looked like a young Michael Douglas, playing the role of an attorney or a banker. The role of a banker was most appropriate. Ron Laitsch owned Authentic Creations Literary Agency. It opened in 1993, and represented more than 70 writers. Aside from the publishing industry, Ron had worked

Ron Laitsch with former U.S. Attorney General
Janet Reno

with Universal Studios, Paramount Pictures and Disney negotiating the sale of movie rights. He had also worked with the National Football League and National Basketball Association. He holds a J.D. Degree from the University of Wisconsin Law School and a B.B.A. Degree from the University Of Wisconsin School Of Business Administration. Ron was licensed to practice law in Wisconsin, since 1970. After leaving private practice, he worked for the U.S. Federal Trade Commission.

Ron was appointed to criminal task forces that are engaged in combating telemarketing fraud throughout the Southeast U.S. These task forces consist of law enforcement personnel from various agencies including the FBI, IRS and the Secret Service. In 1996, he was presented with the John Marshall Award by Attorney General Janet Reno for his efforts in combating telemarketing fraud. Now, he was a literary agent.

He had the New York papers spread in front of him, *The Times*, *Daily News* and the *Post*. Ron started with *The Times*, reading a story about terrorism on the airlines. Great, he thought to himself, especially with a flight to catch the following morning. As he took another sip of his coffee, he glanced out the window. He noticed several pedestrians wearing Yankee caps and jackets in anticipation of the playoffs, which began that night. The Yankees were about to play Oakland. The papers previewed the playoff series differently than in past years. New York is an event town, but New Yorkers viewed the playoffs at Yankee Stadium as a sign that the city was rallying from the terrorist attacks on the World Trade Center less than a month ago. A sellout crowd at the Stadium was going to show the world that New York is nothing, if not resilient and courageous.

Ron was caught looking at a woman outside who had painted her face in Yankee pinstripes, when Chris walked in. There was something about the expression on Ron's face that annoyed the young girl. She flipped him the finger. Chris stood to Ron's left for a good 30 seconds with no acknowledgment, even though he was chuckling. He arrived in time to watch Ron and the girl outside.

"I think she likes you," Chris said, startling Ron.

Ron looked like a man who had just awakened from a dream.

Chris was wearing the usual old barn jacket and Levi's jeans, but with a blue sweater and collared shirt. That was Chris' idea of dressing nice. He ordered a regular coffee from the woman with the nasal voice and frowned when he saw the no smoking sign. Coffee and cigarettes go together like Siegfried and Roy, Chris thought. He shook his head and grumbled something.

"Good trip?" Ron asked.

Chris had taken Amtrak from the station in New London, Connecticut, to New York, which was about a three-hour-ride.

"Amtrak did away with the smoking car," Chris replied. "I should have arranged for a limousine."

Ron shrugged his shoulder. "No smoking in the limos either."

Chris pointed to the window to the sight of the bumper-to-bumper traffic outside, struggling to move down the crowded Avenue of the Americas.

"The whole world is choking on smog. Nobody seems to give a damn. But God forbid you should light-up a cigarette."

"Maybe you should quit smoking," Ron said.

"Maybe I should get another agent," Chris retorted, with a half smile.

For a second time, Ron shrugged his shoulders.

"I'd be happy to write you a reference."

Finding a new agent was a standing joke between Chris and Ron. In reality, the two were inseparable. They were as close as brothers. They often bickered like two brothers. Much like the day when Chris and Debbie first met, this was a *Jerry McGuire* situation. Ron was the struggling agent, paying the price for having a conscience, when he and Chris first met. As a writer, Chris was the outrageous fictitious receiver for the Arizona Cardinals, a role played by Cuba Gooding Jr., who refused to "dance" for anyone on the field, especially with editors. Those days were long gone. Ron now handled names that were legendary in the motion picture industry and in sports. Chris was still somewhat peculiar, but had learned how to be a team player.

"Now, could we get to business?" Ron said, setting his black attaché case on the linoleum table.

He pulled out a stack of papers and handed them to Chris, who was now seated with his back to the window.

"This is your appearance schedule for the promotion of the Frankenstein and Dracula books. You've got three weeks of books signings with *Borders* and a convention during the last weekend of October. You're also going to be given an award at a horror theme restaurant here in New York. It's called the Frankie or something like that. You also have a lecture to give at Princeton."

Chris flipped through the pages. The second sheet contained a list of dates and locations for the book signing tour.

"Connecticut – New York – New Jersey. . ." Chris mumbled to himself, as he scanned the list. He glanced back up to Ron. "This is a pretty tight schedule. . . a lot of ground to cover in just a couple of weeks."

"True, but I have to agree with Simon and Schuster publicity. We've got to get to these places in October for Halloween. People aren't going to care about Frankenstein and Dracula at Christmas."

"You're coming with me, aren't you?"

"Tell you what, I'll be there for you at the convention and the award," Ron answered. "I'm going to have to put you on your own for the book signing tour. I've got a project in development that's going to eat up most of my time over the next couple of weeks. But I'll be checking in on you while you're on the road."

Chris looked at him curiously. "What kind of a project?"

Ron floated the idea of a sequel to *Paper Lion,* the old George Plimpton novel about how he spent time in a training camp one year with the Detroit Lions. All the changes in football, better athletes, advancements in technology, would make it an instant hit. People worship pro athletes. They do things on a grand stage. So what would happen if a regular guy spent some time as a player with an NFL team? The outcome would be hilarious, as well as insightful.

Chris liked the idea. "Have you gotten anywhere yet?" he asked.

"Not yet," Ron answered, motioning to the woman behind the counter to bring him another Mocha-Kenya.

She walked over with a fresh pot. Oh, the smell of the fresh brewed Java. Chris wanted a cigarette. He even thought of telling the indignant patron who would inevitably complain to go call security if they'd like to.

"One of the 30 teams out there would have to be interested," Ron said. "The writer might be harder to find. He'd have to be younger and in good enough shape to gets his brains beaten in a few times, not to mention the workouts. I was hoping that you knew someone."

Chris chuckled. "A young writer in shape? Does such a guy exist? I wouldn't get your hopes up, but I'll ask around."

Ron stood up and donned his trench coat again, looking like a police detective. He shook Chris' hand, and thanked him for helping to find a writer for the *Paper Lion* book. Then he headed out the door for his meeting with an editor at Simon and Schuster. Chris had to use the restroom before leaving for Penn Station and the trip home. Then he walked outside, holding up his right arm to hail a taxi. A cabbie drove by, then rammed on his brakes. Suddenly, he had room for a passenger.

"Where to, Mr. Simms?" the cabbie said, as Chris slid into the back seat.

"Pardon me?" Chris asked, appearing bewildered.

"Aren't you Phil Simms?"

"Uh, no, I'm not," Chris replied, half smiling.

"You're not Phil Simms?"

"No, I'm Chris Schildt, the writer."

The cabbie, who wore a Giants cap, had a white beard, neatly groomed and a pair of thick glasses. He had a New York accent– Central Park sounded like Central Pawk. He wasn't interested in the fact that Chris was a writer.

"A writer? My ass! Figures, my chance to meet someone important and what do I get stuck with, a writer! Where to?"

"Penn Station, if it's not too much trouble," Chris said, annoyed.

He had been approached more times than he could remember by people mistaking him for Simms, even with the extra pounds he was lugging. They must have thought that Simms had put on a lot of weight. Chris had been asked for his autograph on countless occasions. Phil Simms was a legendary player that Chris greatly respected. He never once considered passing himself off as the real quarterback from the Giants. The cabbie was the only person that Chris had ever encountered that actually was rude to him when he told the truth about who he really was. The cabbie didn't say another word for the entire trip. When he screeched the cab to a halt in front of the station, Chris left him a nice tip, which surprised the driver. Chris walked down a few levels to the tracks and found the train bound for Connecticut.

When he took his seat on the train, Chris considered taking a nap. The ride through the city was interesting enough the first time, but after that. . . And then there was Connecticut. Riding by the stations in Greenwich and Fairfield, looking at the parked luxury cars that most people couldn't afford. Then there were the dingy cities of Bridgeport and New Haven after that. Beyond New Haven was the beautiful countryside and foliage again.

Chris thought about his hectic book signing schedule as he dozed off eventually waking up again in Guilford, a Connecticut shoreline town about 20 minutes east of New Haven. He was still about 45 minutes from a cigarette. Soon, though, he was lost in the view. The train zipped along, creating a blur of trees. Most of the time, they resembled a line of endless green, but in the fall the red, orange and yellow leaves looked like a streaming rainbow. Chris finally arrived in New London shortly before three in the afternoon, where Debbie waited patiently in front of the station for him.

CHAPTER FIVE

The Crystal Mall in Waterford was approximately four miles from Chris' house, making it convenient for occasions such as buying a birthday gift for his nieces, Alyssa and Heather. Chris had been driving with the window down. It was an especially warm fall day. Having the window down made it easier to smoke. He didn't have to blow the smoke around the inside of his beloved '89 Jeep Islander, stinking up the interior with a smell that was nearly impossible to get rid of.

Shopping for Chris was normally a regimen. The idea was to get in, buy it, then get out as fast as possible. Don't window shop, and avoid bumping into people he knew. However, this particular shopping trip made it hard to keep to the rules. He had no idea what to get. Alyssa and Heather wanted a Barbie doll, but gave no further specifics. So, shopping today meant rummaging through the endless rows of Barbie's, trying hard to remember the ones Alyssa and Heather already had. Normally, he would have sent Debbie to grab something. But Alyssa and Heather were his favorites, his "little angels." He loved them as if they were his own.

After he parked the Jeep, Chris headed for the main entrance of the mall between Sears and a hip restaurant / bar called Charlie's. As he walked down a lane he saw a man who he recognized as Arnie Hull, a guy he played football with at East Lyme. Arnie was walking with a young looking woman.

Arnie was still tall and thin, just like he was back in high school, shaped like six o'clock. He wore light blue oxford khakis with no socks and a pair of docksiders. He had a sweater tied around his shoulders. Arnie looked pretty good for his age, even though his salt-and-pepper hair was thinning. The woman who was walking with Arnie had shoulder length auburn hair. She was wearing a red blouse, black slacks, heels and rings on both fingers and pinkies. They were headed to a white sports car, a BMW Z-3 Roadster. It looked brand new.

Chris could hear them arguing, something to do with their Visa card, and how it was being used too much. Arnie asked her if she could possibly go a day without shopping. When they reached the car, Arnie dumped four Macy's bags into the trunk. Chris walked over to him, excited to see someone from the old team. He wanted to say hello.

"Arnie? Arnie Hull?" Chris said, with a pleasant smile.

"Do I know you?" Arnie replied.

"It's me, Mike Schildt." Chris figured that Arnie would know him better as Mike. Chris went by his middle name back in high school. He thought it sounded tougher than Chris or Christopher.

Chris extended his right arm to shake his hand.

"Mike Schildt?" Arnie squinted his eyes, appearing confused, using his right hand to extend his glasses to take a closer look "Sorry, But I don't remember you."

"I was a defensive back," Chris said. "Our lockers were next to each other."

The woman with Arnie had already seated herself in the passenger side of the Beamer. She stared at Chris through the driver's window, appearing to study the way Chris was dressed with his old blue jeans and sweatshirt. She had a sour expression on her face.

"I played for East Lyme," Arnie said. "I remember all the guys I played football with. I don't remember a 'Mike Schildt.' Now, if you'll please excuse me, I have to be going."

Arnie shoe-horned the last bag into the trunk. He slammed

the lid shut, then walked around Chris and got into the car. Chris looked at him, confused. *How could he not remember me*, he thought to himself. As he stood in the same spot, Arnie started the car and rolled down the window. It was obvious that the conversation was over.

"Arnie, it's me. . . Mike," Chris said, putting a hand on the car, as he bent over to look at him closer. "I'm the guy who got hurt. I was in the hospital. . ."

"Hey! I said I have no idea who the hell you are!" Arnie said angrily. "If you're looking for a handout, or something, you're wasting your time. And get your hand off the Roadster. You're smudging the wax!"

As Chris slowly pulled his hand away from the Beamer, Arnie shot him a dirty look. He mumbled something. Long after the BMW left the parking lot, Chris just stood in the same spot. He couldn't believe what had just happened. He forgot all about the birthday gifts eventually limping his way back over to the Jeep, then headed for home. He didn't even think to light a cigarette.

Chris had the house to himself when he returned. He walked into his office and dropped down in the chair at his desk. The phone next to the computer monitor on top of his desk rang. He ignored it. Chris just sat in the chair, staring out to space with an empty look on his face. He slowly opened a desk drawer, carefully moved papers aside, until he found an old color photograph. It was a picture of him in his East Lyme football uniform. The boy in the picture wore number 72, and a broad smile. His bright, blonde hair was parted on the right. The picture was taken of him wearing his maroon jersey, which the Vikings used for home games. He spent several minutes studying the old, faded picture, in a brooding silence. A good 15 minutes passed, staring at the photo. Chris finally stood up and reached for his barn jacket. It was a little later in the day now, and was quite cool outside. He slid the picture into a top pocket of the coat, grabbed his keys and headed for the Jeep.

Chris drove to New London to an abandoned building on a dingy street of rundown homes, just off the downtown area of the city. The building used to be a boarding house, where Chris lived as a teenager, when he had the money for rent. It still looked the same, a yellow house, with three floors and lots of windows, although most of the glass panes were smashed out. Chris pulled the Jeep in front of the building, parking under a sprawling oak tree. There was a broken sidewalk that led to the front steps and a decaying porch. The door was sealed off by a sheet of aging plywood, and a white sign with bold, black letters that read Condemned.

He took the picture out of his barn jacket and rested it on the second step with the image facing out. The wind blew it over a couple of times, but Chris kept picking it up and placing it upright again, so that he could see the face staring back at him. Then he took several steps backwards, and sat down on a tree stump a few feet away. Traffic zipped along the street behind him, yet he heard nothing. A stray cat hopped onto the railing that outlined the steps, then scurried through a broken window, but Chris didn't notice it. His attention was fixed on the image of the boy in the picture.

He looked into Mike's eyes with a solemn expression, whispering, "I suppose you saw what happened the other day at the high school. I can only imagine what you must be thinking, and how much of a disappointment I am to you. A fat, lazy old man, right? Is that what you think of me? You're sadly mistaken, old friend. Don't let the house, the swimming pool and money fool you. You see, the pain that *you* experienced became *my* nightmares. There isn't a day that goes by that I don't think about how it used to be. The cold. The hunger. The tears. The never ending pain. I know how frightened you were. I remember it well. For you, it's all over. I'm the one who has to carry it with me for the rest of my life.

"But what I don't understand is why didn't you ask for help? Someone? Anyone? Don't you dare tell me that you didn't need anyone's help? Remember who you're talking to. You can fool everyone else, but not me. You weren't as strong as you would have others believe. You can't tell me that you didn't care about anyone or anything. I know better."

Out of the corner of his eye, Chris noticed a young boy, no older than nine or ten, staring at him. The child, an African-American, wore an old pair of black sweatpants, ripped at the knees. He had a tattered red t-shirt. No coat. No hat. There was nothing to keep him warm.

"You okay, Mister?" the boy asked.

Chris slowly turned to look at him from where he sat on the tree stump, but said nothing. His face was void of an expression.

The boy looked at him curiously. "You okay, Mister?" he asked again.

Chris answered him with a solemn nod of the head, but still said nothing.

"Who are you talking to?" the boy asked, turning his head from right to left to take a look around.

Chris shrugged his shoulders. "Nobody, I guess."

The boy threw him a warm smile. "Don't feel bad. I talk to myself sometimes, too."

Chris nodded his head for a second time, staring down at the ground beneath his feet.

"Who's the guy in the picture?" the child asked, pointing to the photograph on the steps of the old boarding house.

"Someone I used to know a long time ago," Chris mumbled, his voice closer to a whisper.

"A friend of yours?"

For the first time since the boy emerged from out of nowhere, Chris smiled. "You might say that. Actually, he was the only friend I had, a long time ago. He even saved my life once when I was sick in the hospital."

The boy's eyes grew wide, and his expression turned more serious. "Wow, that's a mighty big favor. I hope you did something nice to thank him."

Chris' smile faded. "No, I never did," he replied.

The child released a whistle, shaking his head. "Man, you should have done something like Mrs. Williams. . ."

"Mrs. who?"

"Mrs. Williams, my neighbor over there," he replied, pointing to a rundown house across the street. "Mr. Williams was sick once, and I mowed the lawn for them. Mrs. Williams knew that I liked birds, so she gave me this."

The child reached underneath his T-shirt and pulled a silver chain with a large medallion. There was an image of what appeared to be a falcon rising up from a bed of fire.

"I don't know what kind of a bird this is, but it doesn't matter. I just like birds."

"May I see that?" Chris asked, staring at the image on the medallion.

The boy shrugged his shoulders. "Sure," he said. He pulled the chain over his head, and then handed it to him.

Chris studied the image for minute, and then smiled. "This is not just a bird. It is a *very* special bird," Chris said, smiling warmly. "It's called the Phoenix, and a long time ago, the ancient Egyptians believed that the Phoenix was a bird that lived in the desert for over 500 years. Then it set itself on fire, and arose from the ashes renewed, reborn, young and strong again. But remember, it's just a story. I don't want you to ever play with fire."

"I don't play with fire!" the child replied sharply.

Then he walked over to the steps of the abandoned boarding house and retrieved the old photograph from high school. He brought it over to Chris, saying, "Since this guy is wearing a football uniform, he must like football. Maybe you could get him a football or some tickets to a game."

Chris appeared not to hear the boy, as he stared at the medallion. When the child repeated himself, Chris' eyes slowly drifted up to glance at the picture. After a few minutes, Chris reached up to take the photo from the child's hand. His eyes danced back and forth, looking at the image of himself in his East Lyme uniform and the image of the Phoenix engraved on the necklace.

Suddenly, Chris smiled. It was a robust smile.

"What's your name?" Chris asked the child, and there was a tone of excitement in his voice.

"Jerome," he answered, and then pointed to a house to the left of the abandoned building. "I live in that house over there."

"Someone once asked me if I believed in angels. I said no, I don't," Chris said to the child.

He stared down at the picture and the necklace again, whispering something about *the Phoenix* and *Paper Lion*. Then he glanced at Jerome again, with a broad smile. "You know something, Jerome, after meeting you, I've changed my mind."

Jerome answered Chris with a smile of his own.

Chris handed the necklace back to the child, and then reached for his wallet in the back pocket of his jeans. He quickly thumbed through the thin stack of bills. He turned to Jerome and asked him if he'd like to earn $83. It was all the money he had with him.

Jerome looked at him suspiciously. "Doing what?"

"I'd like you to make a telephone call for me," Chris said.

"That's a lot of money for a phone call," Jerome replied.

"Well, it's a *very* important phone call," Chris said, handing him the cash.

"OK, I can call from my house. Who do you want me to call?"

Chris reached into the pocket of his barn jacket for his cell phone. Then he scribbled out a message on a piece of paper and a pen that Chris had in his jacket.

"I'll dial the number," Chris said, handing Jerome the message. "The person you're calling is Ron. When Ron answers the phone, give him this message."

Chris dialed the number, then held the phone up to his ear. "It's ringing," Chris said, quickly handing the cell phone to the child.

The child held the phone to his ear with one hand, and the note in the other. After a couple of seconds Jerome said, "Ron, my name is Jerome. I'm a friend of Chris, the writer. He said to tell you that he found a football player for you. He said to tell you that his name is Mike."

CHAPTER SIX

The boys, who were home for the weekend from school, were still asleep when Chris awakened at 6 a.m. for a morning run. Running was always more of a means than an end, to Chris. You run to get to first base or to catch a bus. Today, however, on a chilly, peaceful Saturday, with a touch of fog rising and dew on the grass, running was its own end. At least that was the plan. So Chris, wearing a new pair of white sneakers, old gray sweatpants cut off at the knees and a torn blue sweatshirt, embarked out the front door, shading his eyes from the sun with his tattered blue University of Connecticut baseball cap that he wore for luck It turned into more of a run/walk/stumble/sick to your stomach/feel like passing out on the asphalt experience. It was early enough where not many of the neighbors were up to see Chris' midriff jiggle. Chris had hoped to make it to Leary Park, the centerpiece of the Village, a few miles from the house. He made it down Beacon Hill to Grabner, maybe a mile in total, then decided Leary Park would have to wait another day.

As he dragged himself back to the house, Chris would stop occasionally, mostly to wipe the sweat that his cap couldn't contain as it dripped down to his forehead. He would jog for about 30 seconds, then walk. His walk was closer to a hobble, actually, then he'd run for 30 seconds more. The seconds felt more like hours, especially when he started to hyperventilate. When he saw the house from a hundred yards away, Chris decided to go for one last quick sprint. That lasted for about 50 feet, then it was back to hobbling again.

When Chris finally reached the house, he burst through the front door huffing and panting, scaring the hell out of Chris Jr.

and Dan, who heard the commotion from the family room. They jumped to their feet and stared at the door. Chris was gasping for breath and coughing.

Chris Jr. turned to look at Dan. There was a broad smile on his face.

"Now *that* would make for a great Marlboro commercial," he said.

Dan giggled.

"What did you do, walk up the driveway?" Chris Jr. added.

Dan giggled again.

"Funny," Chris replied, still out of breath. "Now help me to the couch."

Dan and Chris Jr. noticed how sweaty he was. They looked at each other with a sour expression, shaking their heads.

"Fine, I'll just drop dead over here."

Chris dropped down on the stairs. As he gasped and coughed, Chris caught a smell coming from the kitchen. It was pancakes, eggs and bacon.

He yelled up the stairs to Debbie. "Why do they always get breakfast cooked for them on the weekends, and I only get cereal?"

Debbie glanced over to the stairs to answer him, but noticed his condition. "What happened to you?" she asked.

"I went for a jog."

Both Dan and Chris Jr. giggled. Debbie was trying hard to keep from snickering.

"You still haven't answered the breakfast question," Chris said.

"They're my babies that's why," she replied with a motherly tone of voice.

"Well, what the hell am I?"

"Right about now?" Chris Jr. looked at him. His smile

broadened. "You're the guy who's stinking up the house."

Chris pulled himself up the stairs on his back, moving like a crab. When he reached the top of the stairs he could see Debbie standing by the stove in the kitchen. She was dressed in a light blue jogging suit. Chris could smell the bacon, and hear it sizzle in the frying pan. He took a long whiff and smiled.

"How would you like your eggs?" Debbie asked.

"Just some wheat toast and a coffee with skim milk, thanks," he replied.

That one slipped out. Skim milk? Chris hated skim milk. It was like drinking water mixed with cardboard.

Debbie looked at him curiously. "Skim?"

"Did I say skim? I must be lightheaded from running."

Debbie poured him a cup of coffee in his favorite mug. It was a chipped old Christmas mug that Chris Jr. gave him years ago. As Debbie walked over to the stairs, he could see the steam rising from the cup. It smelled real good, but not as good as the bacon.

After breakfast, Dan was off to Waterford High School to play football with his friends. Chris Jr. planned to lounge around the house practicing the fine art of doing nothing. Debbie was heading off to the Crystal Mall. Chris showered and shaved, then went to his office downstairs to work on the computer. Actually, he sat at the computer for only a couple of minutes. His back was hurting real bad from the morning jog, as short as it was. The pain was more than he could stand. So he headed upstairs and laid down in bed, falling asleep for about an hour or so. Lying prone was the least stressful position for him. The house was fairly quiet for most of the day, except for the sounds of Chris Jr. thumbing through the channels on the television. The family had a big screen TV with surround sound, the envy of armchair quarterbacks everywhere. A day in front of the television for Chris Jr. was like an entire day at the movie theater.

That evening the family gathered in the kitchen for dinner. No one had noticed that Chris wasn't smoking. The only thing that the boys noted was how irritable he was. They never noticed that the pack of cigarettes that Chris kept by the fireplace was missing. It had been a full day without smoking. It felt like an eternity.

Debbie made stuffed sole for dinner. Chris had one piece of fish, a small helping of potatoes flavored with onion soup and some kind of broccoli washed down with a diet coke. Chris never drank diet *anything* in his life. He had said in the past that it tasted like toilet water. There was no second helping either. This caught Chris Jr. and Dan's attention. They glanced at his plate, then up to him suspiciously.

"Don't feel good?" Chris Jr. asked.

"Do I look sick?"

Chris Jr. shrugged his shoulders. "Just wondering – that's all."

It was Chris' turn to appear suspicious. "Wondering about what?

"Just wondering why you haven't eaten half of the ocean," Chris Jr. answered.

Dan broke out laughing. Even Debbie was finding it hard to contain to a giggle.

"I heard the aquarium wanted to *Free Willie*, but they were afraid you'd eat him," Dan said, jumping in with his brother.

Now it was impossible for Debbie to hide her amusement. Her face turned bright red, and she broke out laughing.

"Let's see how hard you laugh when I forget to pay your tuition bills," Chris said.

"No problem," Chris Jr. replied casually. "We'll just move

back home."

Chris retorted with one of his favorite lectures. "Speaking of college tuition, I don't understand it. My father never gave me as much as a penny for college. I put myself through school, while working full-time as a cop. And I also worked two part-time jobs to raise you kids."

Chris Jr. answered him with a loud belch.

"And he goes to Yale," Chris said to Debbie, pointing a finger at junior.

That was a typical dinner at the Schildt house.

Later in the evening, Chris and Debbie headed up to bed. It was around nine o'clock. Debbie went into her nightly bathroom routine, which usually lasted for an hour. Chris never did understand what anyone could possible do in a bathroom for about an hour, especially just before bed. How long did it take to put on a nightgown and brush her teeth? Certainly not an hour. Still, what a woman did in a bathroom was something that Chris didn't want to know about. He called it the mystique of a woman.

Chris used the time to try and do a couple of exercises before lying down in bed. He put his feet together, bent over, then tried to touch his toes. The tips of his fingers only reached as far as his knees. It wasn't much, but it was a start. As he bent down again, he could hear Debbie opening and closing all kinds of cans and tubes. He figured that he still had plenty of time, so he lay down on the floor on his back. His goal was to do ten sit-ups. Chris raised his knees and lowered his feet. He was trying to do a crunch, which was something he had seen in a Nike commercial. He put the palms of his hands behind his head, and then slowly raised himself up from the waist. Chris felt a lightning bolt of pain from his back that shot down his left leg. He released a loud grunt, loud enough for Debbie to hear him from the bathroom, even with the door closed. She poked her head out the door, and saw Chris lying on his back. He looked at her. She looked at him down on the floor, huffing as if he had just run three miles.

"Are you okay?" she asked.

"Never been better," Chris grunted, grinding his teeth.

"What are you doing?"

"Sit-ups," he said, clearing his throat. "I got in 50."

"The boys are right down stairs. Their going to hear the floor squeaking and think that we're.. . . . well . . . you know."

Chris glanced up at her, smiling. "We're what?"

"You know," Debbie replied, accentuating the 'knoooow' part.

Chris snickered. "We've been married for over 23 years. They know we don't 'you know' with them in the house."

He had no sooner finished speaking when they heard the boys yelling from downstairs. "Gross!"

"Get a hotel!"

"Do you mind? You're making us sick down here!"

It was impossible to say who was saying what. Not that it mattered. Debbie's face turned a bright red. There was an "I told you so" look on her face.

JOURNEY OF A THOUSAND MILES

CHAPTER SEVEN

The distance between his house and Leary Park, and an office that suddenly resembled a gymnasium, this was Chris' universe. And, like the Titans of Greek mythology, Chris ruled his universe with absolute power.

Chris was up at five o'clock every morning, while Debbie was still in bed. His workout program started with a two-mile run. When he returned to the house, Chris ate his breakfast, which consisted of a banana, a vitamin and a high protein drink. Then he went down to his office to lift weights, followed by two sets of 50 crunches. Music blasted through a set of headphones connected to a portable CD player that he wore around his waist. Something like ZZ Top or the sound track from the movie "A Knight's Tale."

Chris' knees and ankles were strong again. He no longer required braces. His arms had taken form with muscle, and his waistline had dropped four inches. In all, he had lost more than 30 pounds. His clothes barely fit him anymore, and he used a belt to hold up his jeans, unlike before, when there wasn't enough room to tuck in a shirt. And he hadn't smoked for the past two months. The only thing about him that was the same as before was the pain in his spine that had grown worse.

Over the past two months, Debbie had grown extremely concerned about Chris' change in behavior. True, he was in better shape. Yet he hadn't written a word since this regimen of exercise began. He didn't seem to care about writing anymore, and he refused to speak to his editor. It was only a few weeks away from Christmas. Normally, Chris loved to help her with the shopping and decorating, but no more. It was as if he had no time for anyone or anything, except for his rigid training program. Often, he didn't even know what day of the week it was. Chris was also watching the football games on television again. He was even taking notes about the various plays. It was as if she was witnessing a metamorphosis that Debbie could not explain, and Chris had no answer for. There was never any mention of *Paper Lion*. Ever since they were married, Chris had shown no interest in professional football whatsoever. He used to get annoyed when her father came to the house for a visit and asked to watch the game on television. Debbie never gave it much thought in the past. She knew of his injury playing the sport, and figured that he didn't need to be reminded of a very difficult time in his life. Chris had refused to allow Dan to play football in high school, except in his senior year. He knew that Dan would spend most of the games sitting on the bench, never having played football before. All that had changed in a very dramatic way.

One day, Debbie stopped by Dr. Doherty's office, without an appointment. She had hoped that he could give her some answers, since Chris' peculiar behavior started after his last visit. The receptionist, a brunette named Lynn, told her that there really wasn't any way for her to see him. The schedule was packed tight. Debbie turned to leave when Doherty happened to step out of an exam room.

He looked at her with a hint of recognition. "Aren't you Chris wife?" he said, his eyes squinted.

"Yes. I was hoping that you might have a minute to spare."

Lynn, the woman at the front desk, quickly turned to the doctor. "I told Mrs. Schildt that your schedule was full."

"I think we have a couple of minutes to spare," Doherty said, with a wink. He motioned for her to follow him to his office.

Debbie took a seat in front of Doherty's desk. The office was spacious, with white painted walls, covered by various diplomas and certificates. The desk was against the back wall, and covered with neat stacks of thick folders. There was a laptop, a telephone and pictures of his family.

Dr. Doherty dropped down in his chair behind the desk. "So what's up?" he said, with a pleasant smile.

"It's Chris," Debbie replied. "Something's wrong."

Doherty's smile quickly faded. He lurched forward in his seat. "What's happened? What's the matter?"

"I'm not exactly sure," she replied hesitantly. "I don't know where to begin."

"Is it his spine?"

Debbie shrugged her shoulders and a tear was forming in the corner of her eye. "It's a lot of things."

"Such as . . .?"

"Well, for one thing, he has been exercising a lot," she said hesitantly.

Doherty stared at her. "I'm sorry, but why would that concern you?"

Debbie shook her head. "You don't understand . . . that's all he does. He doesn't write anymore. He's been ignoring telephone calls, even from his editor. Sometimes he doesn't even know what day of the week it is."

"Has he injured himself recently? A blow to the head?"

"No, no injury. But there's more. . . He doesn't simply exercise, he's obsessed with training like an athlete. He doesn't care about anything, except for exercising. Last week, I woke up early. I saw Chris in the living room. He was actually down on his knees praying. He's never been very religious before. He never goes to church. I didn't hear everything, but I did hear him asking God to help him make his old body strong again, and to help him with the pain in his back. He won't admit it, but he's been in terrible pain."

"You did the right thing by coming to see me," Doherty said, after a moment of silence, as he thought about everything Debbie had reported. "I'm going to schedule him an appointment. It will give me a chance to talk with him. I also want you to schedule an appointment for a complete physical. When he goes, I'd suggest you go along and tell the family physician exactly what you told me. Chris is on heavy medication for his seizures. It would be a good idea to get blood work done. That could certainly be affecting his behavior."

"I'd appreciate it if he didn't know that I came to see you," Debbie said.

Doherty nodded his head, with a reassuring smile. "OK, I'll tell you what. I'll give Chris a call and tell him that I'd like for him to come in for a follow-up on his spine. I won't mention a word. Chris is hitting 45, correct?"

"This January," Debbie answered.

"Well, that could certainly explain some of this. We could be dealing with a mid-life crisis. Even so, we don't want Chris to do something that could hurt him in the process. So, that's what we'll do. We'll get him in for a couple of checkups and take it from there. But if it gets worse, give me a call immediately."

Debbie stood up and reached over his desk to shake his hand. She thanked him, and then left his office.

Doherty continued to sit in his chair, deep in thought. He stared out the window, as he tapped the tips of his fingers against the top of his desk.

"Crazy? Nah. Crazy like a fox," Pat Doherty whispered to himself. Then he chuckled to himself, knowing Chris as well as he did. "What are you up to *this* time, Chris? What are you planning?"

CHAPTER EIGHT

It had been years since Ron Laitsch had carved out the time to enjoy a Sunday with the television and remote. He wasn't sure, exactly, when there were so many pre-game shows to watch, but he flipped through them all, watching former players and coaches break down each game. National Football League games had become once-a-week events. Ron couldn't help but wonder how some of these former athletes, who may or may not have shunned the media after games because of criticism they received, had no problem unloading strong opinions about today's players. That was evident in every pre-game show he watched. Ron settled on the Giants game. It was their first home game since the terrorist attacks. A touching pre-game tribute attracted Ron to the game and he kept watching.

Tiki Barber, the Giants' running back, scored a touchdown in the second quarter on a nifty, 14-yard running play. Jim Fassel, the Giants' coach, was later seen studying pictures of various formations taken moments before, while discussing them with his players and the coaches upstairs. Ron couldn't help but notice the number of coaches wearing Motorola headsets. *What magnificent advertising*, he thought to himself.

Has any professional game undergone the same technological advancements than football in the last thirty years? Ron thought about the last football novel he remembered that linked the common man to the field, George Plimpton's *Paper Lion*. Plimpton became a Detroit Lions' quarterback during preseason workouts and wrote the now famous novel about life in the NFL on the inside. Clearly, sequel books are successful, considering Chris' triumph with the Frankenstein and Dracula books. What sport was more popular than football? A sequel to *Paper Lion* might be a hit. Football was taking root next to baseball becoming America's co-pastimes.

The game that Ron watched wasn't decided until the last play, when Willie Jackson, a New Orleans' receiver, caught an apparent touchdown pass that would have put the Saints within a two-point conversion of a tie. Jackson was whistled for offensive pass interference because he had shoved cornerback Emmanuel McDaniel out of the way, a replay that television showed from 12 different angles. Ron loved every minute of it.

Football occupied Ron's thoughts from the day he had his revelation with his remote control to the day he received the phone call from little Jerome. Ron was just as excited about the news that Chris had found a writer for the book. That couldn't have been easier. A writer young enough to endure workouts in a physical development center, used by chiseled, professional athletes and savvy enough to write about it. Ron was truly looking forward to meeting this guy Mike. He never suspected that Mike was actually Chris.

Ron had left a few messages with Chris about Mike, but hadn't heard from him in a month. That was unusual. Chris had always kept Ron abreast of everything, especially now, with working on his third monster book. It was to be a sequel to *The Phantom of the Opera*. Not hearing from Chris in such a long time, and to not return his calls, piqued Ron's interest. It just wasn't like him.

Not long after Jerome's call, Ron drove to Dallas from Atlanta for a business conference. He planned on occupying himself en route to Dallas by contacting some of the NFL franchises, running the idea by somebody in the front office, then deciding which team would best fit the goals of the project.

He would make sure to mention early in the conversation that all proceeds would go to charity. This was a charity project, and no one was trying to get rich off the National Football League or the particular franchise.

Ron learned from years of negotiating with publishers to get the money part out of the way early because that's really what they wanted to know. The first call went to the Atlanta Falcons, mostly because his office wasn't far from the Georgia Dome where the Falcons play. He called the Tampa Bay Buccaneers, the New England Patriots, who were about to win their first Super Bowl, the New York Jets and the Washington Redskins. Before leaving Atlanta, he did some research to find the correct contact people to maximize his time. By the end of the drive, this is how the conversations went. . .

The Falcons: "Sure, you can send a proposal, but I wouldn't waste your time."

The Buccaneers: "Proposal? What was that again? Oh, nope, don't bother."

The Patriots: "No, and don't call back!"

The Jets: "Hey, love the idea, but couldn't sell it to the coaches."

The Redskins: "Paper what? Oh, *Paper Lion,* the paper towels, right? I don't think we use that brand."

Normally, Ron would have been a bit irked, but he figured he still had 25 franchises left to go. Someone *had* to be interested or at least would even remember *Paper Lion.* The novel was a classic. When he got back to Atlanta, he started the next round of calls, but not without more research. The drive back to Atlanta was fairly peaceful. Not much in the way of winter weather on Interstate 20, decent temperatures, and Sinatra on CD. There was something about driving alone with your thoughts, mixed with a little Sinatra in the background.

Sinatra was always soothing. Ron's mind drifted from one project to another, and when he got excessive, out came, "Fly Me to the Moon."

Ron was singing aloud. He went through "My Way," "Luck Be a Lady," "Summer Wind," "The Way You Look Tonight" . . . all his favorites. He thought he sounded especially good. Maybe that was another book idea, agents who become singers. Books a few lounge acts. Gets discovered, and then plays Vegas. The idea was a lot more pleasant than dealing with the Patriots again. As he drove, his cell phone rang.

"Where's Schildt? Is he okay?" That was the first thing Ron heard. It was Chris' editor for the monster books, a man named Harold Hosman.

"What do you mean, is he okay?" Ron replied hesitantly. "As far as I know he's fine."

Ron didn't want to let on that he hadn't talked to Chris for nearly a month.

"Well, where the hell has he been?"

"You know writers," Ron said. "They get on a roll, or in a slump, and they get moody. I'm sure it's nothing."

"Well, tell mister wonderful that I want a call--immediately!" Hosman barked.

Ron gave Hosman the "losing you--bad area" line, then hung up on him. He was enjoying the ride too much to let anyone spoil it. Ron's attention, 15 miles outside Atlanta, suddenly wasn't on getting home, or sleeping in his own bed. He began to wonder where Chris was. Ron dialed his home number at 9:15 p.m. They had to be home, he figured. Ron still got the answering machine.

CHAPTER NINE

By Christmas, Chris was running twice a day. The morning routine had become sacred, but a second workout had been added at night. During the evening, the holiday lights from the Village illuminated the neighborhood, giving Chris the Christmas Spirit. He had never felt better. Quite happily, Chris received new clothes for Christmas. Nothing fit him anymore, now that he had lost almost 40 pounds. He could taste food again. Chris had a new appreciation for those who complained about cigarette smoke in public. He started to smell it everywhere. He was running miles at a time, feeling as though the times when he was short of breath walking up a flight of stairs must have happened in another lifetime. The pain in his spine was still a problem. He knew his back wasn't equipped to deal with a daily pounding of running and weight training. Still, he proceeded.

Chris thought about joining a local gym. He even took a tour once, early in his exercise regimen. Workout places are intimidating, especially to people who looked like Chris did the day he visited.

Chris walked through a reception area, where three desks sat along the wall occupied by personal trainers. To his left was a juice bar, offering a number of healthy drinks and shakes. Chris glanced at the drink list and noticed a number of shakes that were supposed to be good for you, even with peanut butter and chocolate in them. One woman, maybe 40, blonde hair in a ponytail and wearing nothing more than a sports bra, sat drinking something called the Peanut Butter Dream at the end of the bar.

Chris went down a flight of stairs. There were a number of cardiovascular machines in the front of the workout area. It was impressive – technology meets the physiology of the human body. Chris was reminded of his Frankenstein novel. But the more he walked around, the more he wondered if some of the people were there to work out or stare at themselves. A gym was out of the question, he decided. All he needed to see were guys wearing spandex--something like a woman's leotard, to Chris' way of thinking. He never wore leotards before and he wasn't about to start now. Chris' home workout sessions were just fine.

The morning of December 26 came amid a cold spell, even for winter in New England. The daytime temperatures never reached 30 degrees. Chris was careful to dress warmly for the morning run mindful that he'd start to perspire sooner or later, and didn't want to be uncomfortable. Leary Park, about two miles from his house, and the goal from the first day he ran, had become a lay-up. Chris had been running to the park, first through it, and then around the neighborhood. The morning run was moving along smoothly as Chris entered the park. It was close to dawn's first light. Chris always tried to keep his mind occupied as he ran, focusing on the weather today. He thought it a bit strange that it was nearly January with no snow on the ground when he suddenly grew dizzy. Chris figured that he might be overdoing it a bit, given that his rhythm had been interrupted over the holidays. It was visit here, visit there. Eat this, eat that. And no time for exercise.

Chris decided to take a break on a park bench to catch his breath. He didn't want to sit too long. The perspiration would make him cold. So he only waited a couple of minutes, then he shot back to his feet, and began running again. The dizziness got worse, and he dropped to the ground, not more than 50 feet from the bench where he sat to catch his breath. There was a stabbing pain in his chest. He started to cough, and blood trickled from the corner of his lip, and down his chin. Soon, his mouth was filled with the salty taste of blood. The pain in his chest grew worse, and he was bleeding internally.

He didn't know what to do. Chris didn't have a cell phone with him, and the park was empty. No one would be at the park this early in the morning, especially on the day after Christmas.

Chris raised himself up to his knees and clutched his chest. He felt terribly cold. After a few minutes of rest, he managed to get back on his feet, and staggered back towards his house. During the long and agonizing walk, Chris would occasionally fall down on the street. Blood completely covered the front of his sweatshirt.

When he finally arrived at his home, Chris dropped down on the couch in the family room. He didn't want to tell the family what had happened. Instead, he pulled a comforter over himself to cover the blood-stained shirt, and fell asleep for several hours.

The boys were home from school on break. They spent much of the day watching football, some nondescript college bowl game. Chris Jr. and Dan, who never watched football with their father before, thought it was a bit strange that Chris stayed on the couch all day, not talking that much. Chris did a decent job of giving the appearance that everything was fine. They never knew how sick he was. And when Chris coughed, he turned his head to wipe the blood from his chin. By late afternoon, Dan left the house to help his grandfather at his restaurant in the Quaker Hill section of Waterford. Chris Jr. headed to his bedroom to catch up on some reading. Chris used the occasion to try and make his way to the laundry room for a change of clothes. When he stood up he felt the stabbing pain in his chest again. He collapsed on the floor, hitting the coffee table on the way down.

Debbie heard the crash from the kitchen, and ran downstairs. When she saw Chris lying on the floor, struggling to get back on his knees, she called out for Chris Jr. When he saw his father face down on the floor and Debbie by his side, Chris Jr. made a sprint for the kitchen and called 911.

The paramedics arrived ahead of the ambulance. They took Chris' vitals and immediately injected him with Heparin, a blood thinner used on heart attack victims. When the ambulance crew arrived, they carefully loaded Chris onto a gurney, then spend off for Lawrence and Memorial Hospital in New London.

By the time Debbie and Chris Jr. arrived at the hospital, Chris had already been wheeled to a room in the emergency ward. Debbie gave one of the nurses at admission Chris' insurance information and medical history. Debbie had grown used to seeing nurses and doctors raise their eyebrows whenever they learned of Chris' health issues. It was no different here. Debbie never did get a look at the nurse's name tag, but certainly noticed the look of consternation on her face after the part about epilepsy.

She also told the woman about his spine surgery and the head injury, dating back to when he was a police officer. When they were finished, the nurse pointed to a seat in the waiting room and told her that someone would be out to see her shortly. All that Debbie, Chris Jr. and Dan, who arrived a few minutes later, could do now was wait in silence.

CHAPTER TEN

The waiting continued for Debbie and the boys in the emergency room. An hour had passed and still no word. Debbie was a about to find a vending machine to get a couple of sodas and a cup of coffee when she saw a doctor emerge through a set of double metal doors. He looked young, maybe in his early 30s, with long brown hair and fair features.

"Mrs. Schultz?" the doctor said, finding it difficult to pronounce the last name.

Debbie nodded her head.

"Your husband is doing okay. I think we caught it in time."

Debbie started to cry. The boys quickly joined their mother at her side.

"What happened?" Chris Jr. asked calmly.

"It's hard to tell," the doctor replied. "It wasn't a heart attack. We think it was a blood clot that might have passed through his heart."

"A blood clot?" Chris Jr. said, interrupting him.

"Your father is a lucky man," the doctor restated.

"Can we see him now?" Danny asked.

"I doubt that he'll be very responsive. Sure, but just for a few minutes."

Debbie and the boys followed the doctor into a room where Chris rested on a gurney. He was connected to several tubes and a heart monitor, punctuating the atmosphere with a slow beeping sound. He was wearing a blue hospital gown. The boys had never seen their father look so very frail in their lives. It was a grim reminder that parents don't live forever, and fathers aren't as indestructible as children might believe.

Debbie kissed him on the forehead, and his bloodshot eyes opened. The boys grabbed a hold of his hand. They had never been so very scared in their lives, or so very thankful. Still, they remained calm for their mother's sake.

"How are you feeling?" Debbie asked, fighting back the need to cry. Her voice was soft and low. "Do you feel any better?"

At first, Chris coughed. More blood trickled from the corner of his lip. He smiled. "Are you kidding? I'm a pit bull," he mumbled, smiling. Then he slowly fell back asleep.

The doctor laughed and shook his head. He turned to look at Debbie and the boys. "We're going to admit him. Why don't the three of you go home and get some rest?"

"Can we go with him up to the ward?" Debbie asked.

"Sure. An orderly will be coming in a little bit to wheel him up. In the meantime, you guys can stay with the pit bull."

Shortly after midnight, the boys took their mother home. It was somewhere around 3 a.m. that Chris awoke in his bed on the cardiac unit. He was alone in a hospital, and for a moment he flashed back to 1973. Chris was lost in time thinking that he was near to death with pneumonia after spine surgery, and he instinctively gasped to breathe through the oxygen tube in his nose. Chris quickly reached for the call button clipped to his pillow. Three nurses came running--a natural reaction on the cardiac unit.

"What is it, Mr. Schildt?" a young nurse asked.

He was still gasping for breath, but the heart monitor showed that he was stable. The nurses looked at each other confused.

"Just relax, and try to breathe normally," one of the other nurses said. She turned to look at the others. "I can't understand why he's out of breath. Better call for a doctor--stat!"

Chris glanced around the room. He looked at the nurses, and he slowly started to breathe normally again. He realized that he wasn't in the Intensive Care Unit from 30 years ago. There was an expression of great relief shown on his face, and he smiled at the nurse who was standing to his right. Her name was Laura, a woman in her 40s, with short black hair and a comforting, motherly demeanor.

"Feeling better?" Laura asked, holding his hand.

Chris chuckled. "Just forgot were I was for a minute. What happened? Where am I?"

"The Cardiac Unit at Lawrence and Memorial Hospital."

Chris stared at her. "Heart attack?"

"A blood clot, but you're going to be fine."

Chris nodded his head. "Good, then get me my clothes. I got to get home."

The nurse looked at him sternly. "You're not going anywhere for a couple of days. So you might as well just relax and see if you can get some sleep."

Chris was about to speak when another nurse stepped into the room. She was carrying a large hypodermic needle in her hand. "The doctor ordered more Heparin."

Chris felt the jab of a needle in his stomach, and his face cringed.

"OK, Mr. Schildt . . . all done," Laura said, squeezing his hand. "We'll get you something to help you sleep."

One by one, the nurses left the room. A few minutes later, Chris heard the sounds of footsteps coming closer his bed. The sound reverberated in his head. The noise was deafening, and it felt as if he was in an echo chamber.

Then he heard a voice next to his bed. "I saw the name on the list in the emergency room. I figured that there couldn't be two people with that name."

Chris glanced up. His eyes were out of focus. Still, he could make out the face. It was Patrick Doherty, his neurosurgeon.

"I'm not in the mood for a lecture," Chris mumbled, then closed his eyes.

"Too bad, you're getting one anyway," Doherty replied. He leaned over the bed, closer to Chris. "You came damn close to making a widow of that wonderful wife of yours. You got lucky this time. . . ."

Chris slowly opened his bloodshot eyes. His voice sounded weak. "I didn't see a light," he whispered.

Doherty cocked his head to look at Chris, appearing confused. "A light? What about a light?"

"The light at the end of the tunnel," Chris joked. "No light means you're going to be okay"

Doherty chuckled, shaking his head. "I wouldn't put that theory to the test again, if I were you."

That sense of amusement from a moment before vanished. Chris grew more serious, eyes staring straight ahead. For a moment, he appeared to be immersed in thought. He was quiet for several minutes.

"There's a strange, yet marvelous event that happens every once and a while," Chris finally said.

Doherty looked into Chris' eyes. "What sort of an event, Chris?"

"For some strange reason, all of the cosmic tumblers fall into place, and at that very moment a door is unlocked," Chris answered, still staring straight ahead, as if he were looking at something in the dull light that surrounded him. "That door opens, and at that very moment the past, present and future all converge, and you see things with perfect clarity."

"What did you see? What was it?" Doherty asked, his voice barely a whisper.

Chris' head slowly turned to where Doherty was standing, next to his bed. He smiled. It was a reassuring smile. "I saw what's at the end of a long, long road. I saw my destiny. And that's why I didn't die 30 years ago. That's why I was never afraid as a police officer. That's how I knew I'd be okay yesterday."

Doherty's voice grew more insistent. "What did you see, Chris? What's at the end of the road?"

Chris' eyes filled with tears, and he was overcome with emotion. "I saw a cold and harsh world that man was meant to inhabit. Cold and barren, yet so very, very beautiful. I had never witnessed such beauty. And I am floating there in that strange place--alone, but I'm not afraid. No, instead, it's a moment of great peace and joy. It's the sort of peace and happiness that I have never known before. Time, place and material things lose all their significance there in that strange, but wonderful place. None of those things matter. Everything else that I have experienced, or have yet to experience is just a fleeting moment along the way, down that road." Chris paused, and his smile broadened, even though he continued to sob. "That's what I saw when the door opened. That's what waits for me at the end of the road. That's why I'm never afraid."

Doherty was finding it nearly impossible to speak. For strange reason, Chris' words carried a degree of truth and meaning. When he was able to speak he asked, "When did this door open for you?"

"When I was a boy, hiding in the closet of my bedroom," Chris answered tearfully. "I had forgotten all about it over the years. But just recently I was reminded about what awaits for me on the other side of that locked door. You probably think I'm crazy."

Doherty quickly shook his head to say no, and he meant it.

He thought no such thing at all. With that, the two men elapsed into silence. Not another word was spoken, and all that was left was two lone silhouettes in a dull island of light in an otherwise dark room.

CHAPTER ELEVEN

There was almost as much comedy as there was irony during Chris' first week home from the hospital. The same guy who used to invent ways to sneak cigarettes suddenly had to get devious about exercise. Chris thought that might make a good topic for one of those daytime talk shows: Husbands who exercise behind their wives' backs.

Nonetheless, Chris played the dutiful patient while Debbie was in the house, even milking a bit of sympathy from her. She'd bring him coffee while he relaxed on the couch with an afghan to keep warm and the remote to keep him company. Debbie thought his days might be lonely at home while she was at work. Husbands have a tendency to do that, to play the sick child in need of his mother. What Debbie didn't know was that Chris had resumed exercising with the same kind of passion as before his sudden illness. There was no way that Mike would have sat like an invalid, and neither would Chris. So it turned into a game: He knew exactly when she'd leave the house for work. He would wash and dry his sweaty clothes without her knowing it then be back on the couch for her return home for the bed rest that the doctor had ordered.

Chris was thankful for a dry winter with no ice or snow on the roads during his afternoon runs. Jogging in the morning was impossible with Debbie around the house. She would call the house a couple of times a day to check on him. But during the afternoon, he would be asleep or at least he was supposed to be asleep. Actually, he wasn't getting any sleep at all. When he wasn't lifting weights, he was running.

Shortly after 12 during an afternoon run, Chris was moving

up Beacon Hill, not far from the house, when he noticed a little girl who lived a few houses away. She was playing with the Christmas lights, turning them on and off in the middle of the day. It looked like she was sending an S. O. S. She was obviously bored with Christmas vacation. Her name was Samantha, 10-year-old busybody of the neighborhood. She was wearing a bright red winter coat that was nearly as long as she was, with a black knit cap. Chris knew her family well, and likewise, Samantha knew that he had just been in the hospital. She was nice enough to Chris when she spotted him running, but nevertheless, she *was* the neighborhood snitch. As Chris jogged past Samantha's house on Beacon Hill, his legs completely gave out, sending him crashing to the ground. Chris was still very weak from the clot. He wasn't injured when he fell, just embarrassed and worried that Samantha might have seen what had just happened.

Samantha giggled. "Are you hurt, Mr. Schildt?"

Chris sat on the ground looking at her. He smiled. "Me? Nah, I'm fine. It didn't hurt a bit."

"I thought you were in the hospital? That's what my mom said."

That one concerned Chris. She saw him running. He figured that, well, yeah, most people in the neighborhood knew he was still running, even though Debbie didn't. But Samantha was a blabbermouth.

"How would you like to earn $5?" Chris asked. He reached into the pocket of his jacket for his wallet. Chris pulled out a $5 bill and held it up in the air.

"I guess so," Samantha replied sheepishly.

"Well, I'm trying to keep my running as a big surprise for Mrs. Schildt," Chris said. "So don't tell her that you saw me running. And you can't tell her that I fell down."

She looked at him devilishly. "You're not supposed to be running because you're sick, right?"

Chris' face soured, as he stared at her.

"I think a secret like that is going to cost $10," she said.

Chris slowly rose to his feet. He brushed himself off, and reached into his wallet for another $5 bill. "Do you know what the word blackmail means?"

She threw him a coy smile and shrugged her shoulders. "Nope, but for $10 I won't even tell my mom that I saw you outside when you're supposed to be home in bed. And you know what a big mouth she has."

"So that's where you got it from," Chris retorted, as he handed Samantha her money. Samantha skipped away, holding the two $5 bills in her tiny hands, as Chris limped back home. He had to make certain to allow himself enough time to take a shower, wash his clothes and get back on the couch. As he neared the door, he coughed a bit, and a tiny stream of blood trickled down from the corner of his lip. The doctor had told him that he could continue to bleed for a while, and that's why he insisted on full bed rest. Chris then felt a sharp pain in his chest. It wasn't nearly as bad as the night he went to the hospital. Still, it hurt him enough to make a short nap somewhat appealing.

CHAPTER TWELVE

Chris had been feeling better when he drove to the New London train station on a snowy February morning, belting out the tune, "I Heard It through the Grapevine." He was singing and bobbing his head back and forth, while drivers of other vehicles had the Texas death grip on their steering wheels. The first snowstorm of the year in eastern Connecticut turned the roads between the Village and downtown New London into a downhill slalom course, but Chris and the Jeep moved merrily along. This would be one of the most significant mornings of Chris' life, or so he figured. Chris was headed to New York for a summit meeting between Mike and Ron. He called ahead to make sure the 7 a.m. train to Penn Station would run on time. New Englanders, despite being used to snowfall in the winter, perfected the art of panic, led by fatalistic weathermen who could make a dusting sound like an apocalyptic blizzard. Still, the train was leaving as scheduled.

Chris went from an oldies station, once Marvin Gaye was finished, to Q-105, an FM station in New London. Frank Carafano, the morning drive host, was one of Chris' favorites. Frank didn't talk too much, so the people who turned on FM to hear music weren't turned off by some unfunny, blathering idiot. Frank usually said just enough and most of it was amusing making every morning an easy, enjoyable listen.

Chris had to keep the beloved '89 blue Jeep Islander home. Heaven forbid any snow or salt marred its good looks. His wife's Grand Cherokee was better in the snow, too. That helped, especially down Route 85 past the mall and toward the highway, where snow plows either hadn't made it that far or had not lowered their plows enough.

Frank had just finished relaying an anecdote, which made Chris chuckle, when he played, “I’m A Soul Man.” Chris loved that one. It was one of The Blues Brothers’ best songs. Chris, like Ron on his drive from Dallas to Atlanta singing Sinatra, had just finished the first refrain of, “I’m A Soul Man,” when he mimicked playing the harmonica, which is a big part of the song. He let go of the wheel momentarily, not a good idea in the snow, and had to do some deft negotiating to make sure the Jeep stayed on course. Despite what had almost been a careening ride, it had been a good morning already. Chris found a parking place on the first floor of the parking garage across from the New London train station. He was actually disappointed he didn’t park on the top floor. He used to dread the walk upon the train’s return, up three flights of stairs, usually swearing out loud because the elevator never worked. Now, he figured he was missing out a chance on quality exercise.

The train from New London to New York usually began in Boston and moved through Providence. Most days, it was packed. But today, the train was beautifully empty. Chris got a window seat neat the café car. He was wearing a new navy blue suit, a red tie and white shirt, which had blue pinstripes. He looked different. The same man, who rarely left the house without a barn jacket, flannel shirt and jeans, the outfit at which Arnie Hull and his bitchy wife smirked, looked years younger. He felt better, except for an occasional back twinge. Chris kind of wished the train had been full, just to show off. He couldn’t wait to see the look on Ron’s face. The ride to New York always made Chris a bit wistful. It was a two-and-a-half hour montage, mostly of the Connecticut shoreline, where haves and have-nots are separated by only a few miles. From New London to

New Haven, it was fairly uneventful except for the section the train went through in East Lyme. It passed mostly through Niantic, a quaint section of East Lyme with a cute downtown full of shops and eateries. Niantic even had a bit of charm, Chris thought, which was more than he could say for the rest of East Lyme.

After New Haven, which was a major stop, the remaining 90 minute ride to Penn Station was a Chris Schildt biography. It encapsulated his old life, especially the rundown buildings and projects of Bridgeport, although the new baseball stadium and arena the city just built could be seen from the train now and looked sort of promising. Still, it was a safe bet nobody else on that train was better acquainted with what Bridgeport offered. Chris Schildt had been alone in empty buildings many times in his life, yet not far at all from places that offered the kind of warmth and security for which he yearned.

Bridgeport's neighboring town to the west was Fairfield, the beginning of an affluent string of enclaves that stretched all the way to Greenwich, on the New York border. Fairfield, Westport, Darien, New Canaan and Greenwich, the towns on the shore, boasted some of the most expensive real estate in the country, as did Wilton, Redding and Ridgefield, the municipalities just to the north. Even Norwalk and Stamford, shoreline towns mixed among the Fairfield-to-Greenwich corridor, were a little more urban, but offered homes affordable only to those who had an appreciable number of zeroes at the end of a paycheck.

For Chris, though, the juxtaposition between Fairfield and Bridgeport was fascinating. How close, indeed, lay Bridgeport's tenements to Fairfield's stateliness. And how far apart was the quality of life for most of the people who lived in the respective towns? And there, Bridgeport vs. Fairfield, and all they symbolized, was Chris' old and new life. There wasn't a time on that train he didn't realize it. Maybe that's why the rides were good for him. He always arrived in New York rather appreciative. Today, though, was a bit different. Today was a day to appreciate Bridgeport a bit more, because that's where Mike would have thrived.

Once the train crosses over the state line from Connecticut, riders get a view of one of New York's true eyesores, the old Downing Stadium, where the New York Titans used to play football. New Yorkers joke that it's fitting how a toilet like Shea Stadium, home of the Mets, is located in a place called Flushing. Yet, Shea was the Taj Mahal compared to Downing. It would have been a much better fit at the Meadowlands, home of Giants Stadium in northern New Jersey, an area of swamps and smoke stacks.

Chris, for the moment, didn't see Downing for its depressing state, but for the football field, which, torn up and brown, still existed. Chris saw himself, or at least saw Mike, playing football again somehow, and the process would begin today.

The train rolled in on time, a bit after 9:30 a.m. The snow that was affecting Connecticut was more of an icy mix in the city. Chris didn't care. Ron had arranged the meeting at a coffee shop near Madison Square Garden, which is attached to Penn Station. Chris would have walked if the weather were a bit nicer. He took a short cab ride, hoping against hope that he'd meet the cabbie from a few months back who mistook him for Phil Simms. Chris looked more like Simms than ever now that he had lost 40 pounds.

The cabbie, unfortunately, didn't speak much English. It could have been the real Phil Simms, or perhaps President Bush, and it's doubtful the man would have known. He had light features, looking almost Scandinavian. He spoke with an undecipherable accent. Chris got out of the cab and could see Ron inside. Nothing had changed. Gray suit, light blue shirt, dark tie. Ron's head was buried in a newspaper, coffee by his side. Chris walked in, nearly tiptoeing, just to make sure he'd surprise his agent. Ron was seated at a table near the window because he always sat at the table near the window.

It was a claustrophobic's nightmare there in the coffee shop. Six tables were in back of Ron, all along the window. Only a few feet separated them from the counter, which had 10 occupied seats. There was a giant menu on the wall in front of the counter with all items written on a chalkboard, barely legible. The rest of the walls had impressive New York sports paraphernalia: a Patrick Ewing autographed jersey, an aerial view of Madison Square Garden from 1994 just as the Rangers won the Stanley Cup, Derek Jeter's No. 2 Yankee jersey, Tiki Barber's No. 21 Giants jersey, and then what looked like a new addition: a giant American flag.

Ron Laitsch's reaction was even more priceless than Chris imagined. Ron glanced up from the paper, looked squarely at Chris who remained stone-faced, and went right back to reading. Then, as in one of those classic sitcom scenes, Ron looked up slowly and pensively, as if in disbelief.

Chris grinned.

"What the hell happened to you?" Ron blurted, not knowing what else to say.

Chris' smile broadened, as he extended his hand, and said, "Hi, I'm Mike."

And, right at that moment, Ron put it all together, no roadmap or assembly required.

"You son of a bitch," Ron said with a grin. "I always knew you were crazy, but Jesus, you're CRAZY!"

"Yeah. Ain't it cool?" Chris said chuckling.

The two men sat down and had coffee together. Chris told Ron everything about the last few months. He explained the significance of Mike. He explained why little Jerome made the phone call. He explained the unreturned calls, the lack of writing. He apologized for making Ron take the hit from the publishing house. He talked about the exercise and his family's reaction.

Chris even told Ron something he'd barely admitted to himself: that he was prouder of himself now than he'd ever been before, published novels and heroic police acts aside.

And throughout the conversation, Ron would shake his head and say, "You son of a bitch," every now and then, unable to express enough disbelief. Ron's line of work got him used to writers' unpredictability but this was off the charts.

Chris had finished his second cup of coffee, something he hadn't enjoyed in a while, when he saw Ron's face stiffen. He'd seen that before. That's usually when Ron is about to drop the other shoe.

"I can't let you back on the field," Ron said. "I mean, I can't even begin to tell you how good you look. But any NFL team that learns of your medical history would kick me in the ass and out the door."

Then Ron saw Chris' face brighten, which wasn't the reaction he expected.

"I have medical clearance," Chris said. "My neurosurgeon back home cleared me. In writing."

"Does he want to lose his license?" Ron said.

"Doherty?" Chris said. "He doesn't screw around. He examined my x-ray not long ago, and said that my back looks as normal as it could, given the history. Plus, I told him I was going to do this anyway, whether he liked it or not."

I knew I'd hear that one sooner or later, Ron Laitsch thought.

"I don't suppose you have the letter?" Ron said.

"Not with me, but I'll get it to you."

"You do that," Ron said.

Ron Laitsch tuned out Chris for a minute and had a thought: This could be better than a *Paper Lion* sequel. He would call NFL teams first thing in the morning with a new proposal, the greatest comeback story since Jim Morris, football's answer to Disney's baseball movie "The Rookie." Nope, this was better. Jim Morris never had a fractured spine. He was never paralyzed. Morris wasn't a decorated police officer. No, this was the story that an agent only dreams of.

CHAPTER THIRTEEN

When Chris left the coffee shop, Ron watched him flag down a cab. Chris noticed an old woman bundled up with a long, black coat and a light-colored kerchief, hauling a few shopping bags a few feet away. Chris not only gave her the cab, but helped her load the shopping bags into the trunk. She smiled at him and Chris smiled back. Ron knew the change in Chris wasn't just physical. A few months earlier, Chris would have either pretended not to notice the old lady or would have gotten into the cab with a scowl, muttering about his busy schedule, and that if the cabbie didn't step on it he'd be late for his train.

"That son of a bitch," Ron said, appreciatively staring out the window, shaking his head.

Ron started thinking about his last meeting with Chris in New York City, in early October, when he mentioned the idea of a *Paper Lion* sequel. It had changed a man's life. Ron was never big into what ifs, but he did wonder, *what if I never mentioned a word about it?* Of course, Ron Laitsch was nothing else, if not someone who could generate the big idea. And so he decided that what ifs were a waste of time, particularly with the possibility of a new, massive, and perhaps landmark project. This project could be a beauty: a man who broke his spine playing football returns to the field 30 years later. Not only would it be an inspiration, but any proceeds would go to spinal cord research. Chris Schildt would be the personification of perseverance, a feel-good story in a country that is in desperate need of as many of them as possible. But would a team or even a publisher go for it?

Ron had been through about half of the NFL teams

proposing the sequel, and was met with responses that ranged from Antarctic cold to lukewarm. But, what the hell. He still had half the league remaining, and an even better project to propose.

It took Ron Laitsch about 15 minutes to hail a cab even though he saw a few hundred pass. He was staying at a hotel near LaGuardia Airport, a hefty cab ride from midtown Manhattan, but convenient in the morning, when his flight was leaving early. The rest of the day would be devoted to finalizing exactly what he wanted to say to a representative from an NFL team, and then making the call.

The cabbie who finally stopped for Ron Laitsch wore a green, New York Jets knit cap. He spoke with a New York accent. "That" was "dat" and "these" were "deeze." The man, whose nameplate read 'K.C. O'Neill,' appeared to be as New York as New Yorkers can get.

Ron asked O'Neill what his reaction would be if he were suddenly given the opportunity to spend a preseason camp with the Jets, or whether he'd be interested in reading about another average Joe who did so.

"You kiddin?" O'Neill answered. "I'd love to, so I could call one of deeze here talk shows where the hosts knows everythin' and tell 'em what they don't know."

New York was big on talk radio.

"Would you worry about getting hurt?" Ron asked. "I mean if you had the opportunity."

"Badge of honor," O'Neill answered. "I mean, I drive a cab. I could drive a cab with a broken arm."

Ron hadn't even mentioned that the person who might be working out with an NFL team once had a broken spine. Just the mere idea, and K.C. O'Neill's interest, was enough.

The two men gabbed the whole way to the hotel. O'Neill

admitted he never had a literary agent in his cab before, while Ron said he never had such a lengthy discussion with a cabbie. Ron left a tip that nearly made O'Neill's eyes bulge. The two men shook hands. O'Neill left Ron his card, just in case he was ever in New York again and needed a ride.

Ron settled into his hotel room, the one with a breathtaking view of New York traffic. He pulled out a notebook and began jotting some notes about what he wanted to say to someone from an NFL team. Be totally honest. Be specific about Chris' medical background, and be clear about the money. Forget about the *Paper Lion* idea.

And he began making phone calls. He started with the Chicago Bears. It had been Ron's experience to talk to the head of the public relations department first. He left a message for Scott Hagel of the Bears, and gave him his hotel room number. Ron repeated the process with six other NFL public relations heads. It was that kind of afternoon. Many phone calls, many messages, none returned.

It was a little after six in the evening when Ron decided he'd forego room service in favor of eating in the hotel restaurant. He stepped into the shower, figuring it had been a long enough day, and that he needed a pick-me-up before dinner. It was a typical hotel shower, not big enough and not enough water pressure. What was supposed to be nice, hot and relaxing turned into a rinse off underneath a steady drizzle.

Ron put on some casual clothes, a beige turtleneck, khaki pants and loafers, combed his hair and just heard the hotel room door close behind him when the phone rang. Ron fumbled for his room key that looked more like a credit card, and made a dash by the third ring.

"Ron?" a squelched voice asked. It was Scott Hagel of the Chicago Bears.

Ron was relieved. At least someone called back. He asked Hagel about where the Bears stood on charity projects.

"What do you have in mind?" Hagel asked. And so Ron gave him the story. A poor kid from Florida moves to Connecticut. He has a bad home life, but uses high school football as an escape. It becomes his passion. Defending a pass play at East Lyme High School, he breaks his spine. He is told by the doctors that he'd never walk again. He nearly dies of pneumonia, and he was even given the Last Rights by a priest. The boy fights like hell to keep from dying and to regain the use of his legs. Not only does he walk again, but becomes a heroic police officer and later a published author. Now his dream is to put the uniform on again. He's just lost 40 pounds and is in the best shape of his life. Lastly, all the money from the project goes to charity.

Ron Laitsch told the story without as much as a peep from the other end of the line.

When he finished, Scott Hagel said, "Are you kidding?"

"Nope," Ron answered. "Your time is more valuable than that."

Then the two men talked about Chris' health as it stood today, how he could get medical clearance, and mostly a timetable to get this process moving. Ron explained the neurosurgeon's letter and said the timetable was up to the Bears. Chris was ready.

There was a pause for several minutes. Ron was beginning to wonder if Scott had hung up on him. It had happened before.

After what seemed to be a very long time, Scott Hagel said, "Would you give Chris a message for me?" Hagel didn't wait for an answer. "Tell him I said 'welcome to the Chicago Bears.'"

CHAPTER FOURTEEN

Chris was driving back to the village at the same time Ron Laitsch was talking to Scott Hagel and the Bears. Debbie had dinner ready when Chris pulled into the driveway, but he decided to go for a run first. The roads around Chris' house were snow-covered. He knew if he slipped and landed a certain way that his back might never recover, but that was becoming more irrelevant by the day. He wore the brightest clothes he could find to go running at night, and started down Beacon Hill. He was wearing a yellow sweatshirt and had reflectors attached to his sneakers. Three months earlier, Chris wouldn't have dared wear yellow, fearing he'd look like Big Bird's long, lost cousin.

Chris was becoming a rather accomplished runner. His footwork had become rhythmic, his balance improved. The fear of slipping wasn't nearly as significant to him as the fear of not finishing. His strides were steady and consistent, all the way out to Leary Park. Chris thought about even running to the Crystal Mall one of these days. It was, maybe, five miles from his house on a busy road. But it was a challenge, a new challenge, and Chris Schildt was nothing, if not game to climb another mountain. The news was even better when he got home: chicken for dinner. Chicken with just a few spices. Nothing creamy, no gravy. No heart attack special. He ate a sufficient portion. When he finished, he knew he had a few minutes while Debbie cleaned the kitchen to run upstairs and sneak in a few crunches.

They hurt his back mercilessly. Still, he knew nothing would strengthen his midsection better. He reasoned that the days when his spare tire would add to his back pain had to be ending soon. Chris had no spare tire left, which took the pressure off his lower back.

Chris didn't want Debbie to hear him blasting any music, so he did the crunches on the bedroom floor wearing his headphones. He had a number of CDs from which to choose, but settled on "Beethoven's Symphony No. 9." The ninth symphony delivered the power he needed. His crunches were slow and steady, happening while his eyes were closed, focusing on the music. The back pain was brutal. Still, his focus had to be on the music. He was in the shower by the time Debbie came upstairs. Now he was taking some delight in making her wait to use the bathroom before bed. Debbie had been doing that to him for 20 years. Chris emerged from the bathroom with a towel wrapped around his waist. Debbie realized she really hadn't taken a good look at her husband in a while. He looked like he did when he was a policeman almost 20 years ago: svelte and solid. She was leery about encouraging him because his obsession with exercise was scaring her, but she knew that he had never looked better.

On the following day, the day that would change his life, nothing happened that strayed from what had become ordinary. It was a day of workouts and protein shakes while Debbie was at work. Chris knew Debbie was making steak for dinner, which would be low enough in carbohydrates to be acceptable. He cancelled his evening run in favor of some lifting in his office/makeshift gym. He would pump iron once dinner had settled.

Debbie was using a household cleaner to wipe down the stove that made the entire kitchen smell like ammonia. Hospitals should be as clean as her kitchen, Chris would say. She heard the phone ring. Debbie was used to hearing it ring quite a bit since Chris had been ducking calls from everybody except Ron. That was another thing that made her suspicious. Debbie glanced at the caller ID. It was Ron. It stopped ringing so that meant Chris, or the machine, must have picked up.

Chris had no idea, but Debbie had been listening outside the office door occasionally in recent weeks. Debbie crept downstairs where Chris worked just off the family room. She stood outside and heard nothing, except for what she thought were the sounds of someone sniffling or crying. She immediately knocked on the door. Chris opened it. He took one look at his wife, threw his arms around her, and began sobbing. Debbie was frightened. With Chris, this could have been anything: his back, the clot, the epilepsy, the writing. She had no idea what Chris was about to say.

He looked her in the eyes. There was a broad smile on his face. He cleared his throat, and then rubbed his eyes on the sleeve of his sweatshirt.

"I'm going to the Chicago Bears," he said.

"What?" Debbie whispered.

"The Bears, the Chicago Bears."

This was the second consecutive day a person close to Chris Schildt had an epiphany. First, it was Ron in the coffee shop, who saw Chris' new physique and figured out the significance of Mike and how Chris had no intention of every writing a football book. And now it was Debbie. As soon as she made the connection to football, the last three months explained themselves with prose more pungent than her household kitchen cleaner.

"So, that's what this has been about," Debbie said rhetorically, still maintaining her embrace on him.

"The Bears…my God…the Chicago Bears," Chris marveled, his voice climbing in excitement.

Chris picked up a towel he'd been using for his workouts to wipe his eyes. Debbie had never seen him so emotional.

"You have no idea what it was like in that damned hospital," he said. "I was done with football forever. But football was all I had."

He didn't have to say anything more about the hospital. She understood him. Debbie had lived with it for more than 20 years.

"Deb, I want to hear the sound that cleats make on a cement locker room floor. I want to smell a locker room again. Oh, to hold a helmet in my hands again. Shoulder pads. Just one last time… But most of all, I don't want to be forgotten. I don't want to be thought of as an old man. I want to know what it feels like to be a champion, just once."

"But your health…"

"The hell with my back!" he said. "All my life I've been worried about it. Oh, the hell with it! Doherty says things have healed way better than anyone could have ever thought. I've lived with the pain for so long I'm used to it. If it gets worse, that's a chance I'm willing to take."

"I didn't mean your back," Debbie replied. Now it was her turn to cry. "What about the epilepsy? Your seizures? Remember what the doctors told you after the head injury? They said that one more serious blow to the head and you could be…" She couldn't bring herself to finish the sentence.

Chris looked her sternly in the eyes. "I honestly don't give a damn anymore."

There were several minutes of silence before Debbie asked Chris when he wanted to tell the boys. Chris balked for a minute, finally deciding it would have to be soon. Just not now. Chris loved his boys, but he also knew that if he told them about the Chicago Bears, they might fall down laughing. Eventually, he knew they'd support him, but not without a possible comedy act. The boys were unaware of their dad's lifelong obsession with playing football again.

Debbie had no idea of what else to say. She walked back to the kitchen and poured herself some tea. She had never feared more for his safety, not since the time when he was a police officer.

"When I wrote the screenplay for *Rocky*
I wanted a symphony of powerful men,
...of lonely women,
...of human ships that crash in the night,
...of love,
...of courage,
...of dignity cast in bronze."

Sylvester Stallone

CHAPTER FIFTEEN

At first glance, Chris could be seen standing in his doorway later that week surveying the neighborhood, contemplating the sun rising just above the row of houses that stretched to the horizon. Smoke could be seen rising from some chimneys, disappearing into an azure blue sky, a scene you'd see on some "Best of New England in Winter" calendar.

Chris was standing at the confluence of every emotion he'd ever experienced. Every pain. Every pleasure. Every tear. Every smile. He was the man in the doorway standing at the cusp of a dream, wearing the requisite apparel of the sports franchise that would help the dream come true: a gray Chicago Bears' T-shirt with the word "Bears" written in blue script, outlined in orange, and black shorts with the Bears' logo on the left leg also in orange. Chris bought them online the night he got Ron's call and had them shipped to the house overnight.

Train like a Bear. Look like a Bear. Act like a Bear, he thought. *Be courageous, proud, just like a Bear.*

It was fittingly Bear weather in the Village. Sunny, but with a crispness in the air that caused your breath to look like smoke rising from chimneys when you exhaled. Chris pictured himself not in Waterford, but at Soldier Field during pre-game, a crowd filing in slowly and steadily, a buzz in the air for what was about to happen. It was one of the landmark mornings of his life. He was standing at the doorstep of something once thought to be permanently elusive, knowing the door was no longer locked. The symphony was about to reach a crescendo, and he knew it. This would not be a morning run. This would be a pre-NFL workout. There was urgency. There was glorious urgency. There would be no sweatshirts or long pants. Weather be damned. He was a Bear now, no matter how brief. He was a Chicago Bear.

He left his house, and by the time he reached the end of the driveway, he was on a dead run in almost mythic contrast to the day he began with his run-walk that had him panting only a few steps from the house. He remained dressed in the Bear T-shirt and shorts. No Bear cap, though. No, Chris would never go anywhere without his lucky University of Connecticut baseball cap, which was becoming as good a friend to him as his Jeep or his dog, Monster.

This was the day, Chris believed, to run beyond the Village. He was going to run to the Crystal Mall. This is what a Bear would do. Five miles? In his sleep. The look on his face was a mix of happiness and resolve as he negotiated the twists and turns of Douglas Lane and finally up a small hill to where Douglas met Route 85.

He ran in place momentarily before he could cross the road. Route 85 was quite busy, and he ran with traffic for the next few miles, past many small businesses that dotted the side of the highway. When he got to the Cross Road, which essentially linked Route 85 with Interstate 95, one of the east coast's primary thoroughfares, he paused for a minute at a traffic light. Chris removed his baseball cap, and, unbeknownst to him, steam could be seen rising off his head. There are hundreds of classic NFL Films scenes of football players in cold weather who remove their helmets causing the same effect. Chris looked like a football player.

He reached the mall in a few minutes, negotiating cars in the parking lot, finally running through the main entrance. He slowed the pace a bit and went to the food court, where he sought out a place that specialized in salads and shakes. The line at Burger King was considerably longer. Chris asked for a fruity montage of crushed strawberries, bananas and pineapples to give him a little energy for the run home. He watched the teenager behind the counter carefully to make sure no sugar was added.

Chris was sweating. He didn't want to wait too long for his body to cool down. He gulped the shake down before heading out the door again. The run home was equally exuberant. He went about ten miles total, longer than he ever had, and felt as though he had energy for ten more. That's what Bears did, he figured.

The house was empty when he returned, as it usually was in the middle of the day during the week. Chris saw the message light flashing on the answering machine. He pressed the button and heard Ron's voice, reciting names of great Bears: Halas, Butkus, Singletary…Schildt! He even mixed in a joke about how Chris had once been the "Refrigerator," the nickname for hefty former Bears' tackle William Perry, but had slimmed down enough now to barely be called "Coffeemaker."

Chris grinned. It was all Bears, all the time. And now it was time for the workout. His run had encompassed more miles than it ever had. So, Chris reasoned, the weight-training must be suitable for the NFL, too. The back-stretching exercises seemed to be working since the ten miles didn't make his back feel any worse. Still, he knew the weights might render a different outcome.

But then, who cared? He was a Bear. And Bears play with pain.

The workout area used to be an empty piece of space in his office, just beyond the desk where his computer sat. Now there was an entire workout set with a large machine and some free weights. The office walls, adorned with successes of Chris' past, including posters and plaques from his days as a policeman, and mementos from his Frankenstein and Dracula books, had faded into the background. They hadn't moved. Chris chose to focus on a slogan that was adhered to the back of his office door, noticeable only when the door was closed. In big, black letters with a white background read the words:

"If they are fast, I will be faster. If they are strong, I will be stronger. If they are determined to win, I will be unstoppable -- for I realize there is no tomorrow."

The words had been committed to memory long ago. They were his national anthem. Chris slipped the CD to the original *Rocky* movie into the stereo. He stared at the sign. He read it aloud, then louder. Then came the leg lifts. He added more weight. He did five sets of 10 lifts. Once, he held the weight for a few seconds, using his right hand to feel the muscles in his legs. They had gone from flab to rock in three short months. The bench press came next. It was more than 200 pounds. Again, five repetitions of 20. This was hard. Usually it was no more than three reps, but what could be "usual" about a 45-year-old going to the Bears? He grunted and hollered, not from any pain, but from pure excitement. Later he worked his biceps and triceps. The biceps weren't quite where he wanted them, but had improved drastically from the days of softness when his arms felt like pizza dough.

He took a break for some water realizing his perspiration had soaked through the T-shirt. He would have to wash the T-shirt and shorts later because this would be his official workout uniform. There would be no more workouts without it. Chris went to the kitchen, deciding to have a protein drink after a few gulps of water. He prepared the strawberry-flavored beverage, and before he took the first sip, decided to toast himself.

"I will pump weights like a Titan!" he said, and then downed the protein drink with the merriment that New Year's Eve revelers enjoy midnight champagne.

He got back to the room, though, and realized that most of the workout was over, save the stretching. If he got nothing else from his trip to the local gym, he had studied a few tips from posters hung at various parts of the workout area and locker room. The better you stretch, the less likely you will pull a muscle. There would be no time for injuries.

Chris' stretching was deliberate. He made no sudden moves, respecting his spine. When he was finished, he realized he felt a bit less back pain today than he had in months. Chris was in the shower when Debbie got home. He came walking downstairs in a pair of jeans and flannel shirt. Some things never change except that now, even the new jeans were falling off him. He threw his arms around his wife and told her of the momentous day. She managed a smile, asked Chris what he wanted for dinner, and then one, last question.

"Don't you think it's about time we told the boys?"

Chris nodded. He knew they'd be home for the long, Martin Luther King birthday weekend. That would be the time.

CHAPTER SIXTEEN

The relationship Chris and Debbie had with their boys was to be honored. It was never difficult for the family to talk, even about things that were awkward or embarrassing. There was frequent dialogue and inspiring closeness, yet the boys respected their parents' authority.

Funny, though, now Chris, who lived his life not caring what anybody else thought, was quite nervous about telling the boys about the Bears. Maybe nervous wasn't the right word. It was more a mix of excitement and apprehension.

The boys would arrive Friday night and would leave sometime on Monday, giving Chris a few options. He could spring it on them just as they came through the door, tell them just before they left, or sometime on either Saturday or Sunday, hoping they wouldn't have plans that occupied all their time. He decided on Sunday morning. Chris, who had been thinking about God quite a bit lately, believed his prayers had been working. He believed that only God knew the plan for his life, and the winding, sometimes-uphill, sometimes-down route it had taken. He chose Sunday morning, hoping the kinship with God at that time of week would help.

Of course, the boys had no idea what was coming. Hearing your 45-year-old father tell you he's going to a National Football League team didn't exactly qualify as business as usual.

While Danny thought his dad's new exercise regimen was cool, Chris Jr. had felt a mix of irritation and suspicion – much like his mother. Chris Jr. and Debbie had had a serious discussion at Lawrence and Memorial Hospital the day after Christmas while Chris was being treated for his blood clot.

Chris sat them down in the family room and stood in front of the big screen television. Chris had been watching less TV lately, except for the NFL playoffs, which had featured the Bears until two days earlier when they were eliminated by the Philadelphia Eagles. Still, it had been a landmark season for one of the league's flagship franchises. Not only was Chris going to a team with history that dated back to the great George Halas, but he was going to a hot team, which had awakened feelings in its fans they hadn't felt since the Super Bowl season in 1985.

The Bears played their playoff game that Saturday afternoon. Had the boys been home, they'd have wondered why their father spent it screaming at the television, calling the referees crooked, pacing the floor, and even heaving the remote control a few times off the couch. Unfortunately, Philly had too much Donovan McNabb – the elusive quarterback, who ended Chicago's memorable season.

Chris chose to wear another new piece of Bears' clothing for his fireside chat – a long-sleeve white polo shirt with the Bears' emblem (a "C" that looked like it had been sat on to resemble more of a football shape). The "C" was black, outlined in orange. Indeed, Chris had spent quite a bit of time on the Bears' web site lately buying whatever he could.

He never used to tuck in his clothes, especially polos, which he'd let hang over his waist to hide the baggage. Today, however, he had the shirt tucked into his pair of jeans, which required the belt to be tightened an extra notch.

There were two adjacent sofas in the family room that formed an "L" shape in front of the television. Debbie sat on the one to Chris' right while the boys were in front of him.

"Boys," he said, "I have to tell you something."

Those words could be construed as discomforting to hear from your old man, especially one with a history of back problems, a blood clot that may or may not have healed, and a recent exercise obsession that was, if no other word applied, puzzling to them. Chris Jr. and Dan sat quietly, eyes transfixed on their father.

"I'm going to the Chicago Bears," Chris Schildt said, unable to contain a grin that could have illuminated Waterford Village.

Chris Jr. looked puzzled. "Bears? As in the football team?"

Their dad nodded, smiled, but said nothing.

"That's *so* cool!" Danny replied.

For a minute, Chris thought to himself -- *gee, that was relatively painless*. He sort of blurted out the Bears part, skipping much of the background he planned to share. Chris was thrilled over Danny's reaction, but was concerned that Chris Jr. wasn't as effusive. Actually, Chris Jr. didn't say anything. His father finally explained why he was leery about letting Dan play football until his senior year. He talked to them about the anguish he felt over a shortened career, Ron Laitsch' idea about *Paper Lion* and why he had been exercising like an Olympian. Danny kept nodding his head, hanging on every word. Chris Jr., meanwhile, was doing a slow burn. He was still a little steamed over the lack of explanation from the night at the hospital. He figured his father was going through a mid-life crisis. He cared deeply about his dad and his mom – worried terribly over what another injury might do to their future.

"Why are you doing this?" Chris Jr. asked. "I mean, what about your back? And your head?"

It was the first occasion for Chris not to smile in days.

"I never *did* get the opportunity to finish my last season of football. And as far as getting hurt again … well, it's better to die on your feet than live on your knees."

Danny loved that one. It was, however, the "die" part that Chris Jr. didn't want to contemplate.

Chris was about to say something else, when Debbie cut him off.

"You might as well back him," she said. "You're not going to stop him."

"A pit-bull, right, Dad?" Danny said, with a grin.

Even Chris Jr. managed a flickering smile. Chris got up and hugged his father. It's doubtful he approved, but if he knew nothing else about his father, he knew one thing – there was no stopping him.

CHAPTER SEVENTEEN

The excitement over the Bears and the anxiousness stemming from how he'd deliver the news to the boys helped Chris forget about his appointment with Patrick Doherty. The doctor, who suspected Chris wasn't just having a midlife crisis the day Debbie went for some advice, told Chris he wouldn't approve any medical clearance for football until he gave him a complete checkup. Chris had no choice but to agree.

Two days after he told the boys about the Bears, Chris drove the Jeep Islander to Doherty's office for the physical. The Islander didn't have a CD player, so Chris bought one so he could blast his favorite music from the 60s and 70s. "We Will Rock You," by Queen.

Dr. Doherty was a few minutes late for the appointment. He had only spoken to Chris by phone, and hadn't seen him since December when he had visited him in the hospital. He stepped into an empty office, yet before he could sit down, Doherty walked in behind him. The doctor's eyes were wide with surprise. He hurried over to Chris to shake his hand. It wasn't merely the 40 pounds he lost that was so impressive. Chris had changed the shape of his body from dumpy to athletic. In five months, he looked 10 years younger.

Chris told him the whole story, beginning with his last year playing football in high school and detailing his injury. It was the catalyst for the radial change in Chris' life.

Chris was careful not to volunteer too much information about his back pain. The exercise made the rest of his body feel better, but made his spine feel worse. As far as the doctor knew, the pain had been lessened because of the weight loss. Still, Dr.

Doherty was going to take every precaution before possibly letting some 300-pound lineman body slam his patient.

Everything about the checkup had gone swimmingly. There was a tap to the knee here with a rubber hammer, and a tap to an ankle there. Then came the spinal x-ray. And that's when Dr. Doherty knew that continued exercise would cause the back to worsen and result in more pain. Chris had neither the strength nor the flexibility in his spine that most 45-year-olds did. Of course, most 45-year-olds didn't have the body Chris did.

Doherty told Chris that if he was insistent on training the way football demanded, the spine would need more elasticity. This meant a series of spinal injections at the pain clinic across the street at Lawrence and Memorial Hospital. It was an outpatient surgical procedure.

Chris was worried about getting steroids injected into his spine, between the joints and the bones. As if that didn't sound daunting enough, Chris had an opportunity to see one of the needles, which was longer than a football. He was concerned over the word "steroids." What if he were drug-tested before camp?

"It's not *those* kinds of steroids," Dr. Doherty said.

Chris scheduled three sessions, two weeks apart. He was told that eating, sleeping and certainly exercising would be nightmarish a few days after each injection. Chris barely heard the words. All he could think of was the saying on the poster he had on the back of his office door, which ended in the words,"...I will be unstoppable, for I realize there is no tomorrow." *If it has to be steroid injections, then bring 'em on,* he thought to himself.

Chris scheduled the first session for the end of that week, believing the quicker he could finish getting them, the quicker he could begin regular training again.

Ron Laitsch, meanwhile, had called the local newspaper, *The Day*, to arrange a phone interview with Chris for the end of the week, which was only two days after the injection.

There were a couple of days between the appointment and the first needle.

Chris trained harder than ever. He also experienced more back pain than ever. For the first time, he felt a twinge in his lower back during leg lifts. The twinge degenerated into a new experience in pain when he lay on his stomach and did the strengthen-the-hamstring routine. Chris lay face down on a bench with the weights at his feet. He slid his legs under and lifted the weight at his heels using his hamstrings for strength. The exercise worked fine for his legs, except that the leg-lift motion he was using must have caused something to press against the spine, resulting in a shriek that would have made Debbie come running had she been home.

Pain, Chris decided, was only temporary. If Dr. Doherty was correct, Chris would not be able to exercise for a few days after the injection, making double running and double lifting sessions necessary for the days leading to the first injection.

Chris wasn't saying much to Debbie that wasn't thoroughly upbeat. He didn't want her to suspect the pain in his back was worsening. Debbie drove Chris to the hospital that Friday for the first injection. Chris' nervousness came not over the pain of the needles, but how long he would be incapacitated. The more days he couldn't fill with exercise, the less prepared he would be for mini-camp.

After he checked into the hospital, Chris was given a gown to wear before walking into what looked like an operating room. He was lay face down on a table as a young looking doctor stepped through a double set of stainless steel doors.

Chris was given a local anesthetic to make the injection of

the long needle into the skin less painful. But when the needle entered the joints between the vertebras of his spine, the agony caused his face to wrinkle. He wanted to cry, but instead released only a series of long grunts. The procedure only took about fifteen minutes. The ride home was mercilessly painful. Had Chris taken the Islander, he might not have been able to shoe-horn himself into the driver's seat. The Grand Cherokee, at least, offered a little more room. Debbie drove as slow as possible, making the occasional bump in the road or sharp turn less painful. For the remainder of the day, Chris couldn't eat nor could he sleep. Yet if the nausea weren't uncomfortable enough, the steroids were causing occasional chills and hot flashes. The first night home, Chris went from shivering under a blanket on the couch to wanting to strip naked.

This was becoming increasingly difficult for Debbie to handle. The exercise and the blood clot were bad enough – and now this. They were shooting steroids straight into his body. She was beginning to wonder if this would ever end. Still, Debbie tended to her husband as best she could, although the nausea, chills and hot flashes came with no warning. Chris had to sleep on the couch with his legs propped up to ease some of the pain. And that was just the first night.

Doherty called the next day to check on him.

"How long is this supposed to last?" Chris asked, and then told him about the side effects.

"Two or three days," Dr. Doherty answered. "But on the fourth day, don't make like you're Carl Lewis. You're going to have to ease into it."

"And by then, it'll be time for another shot, right?" Chris said.

"Unfortunately," the doctor answered before hearing a "click" on the other end.

On the following day, Chris had forgotten about the newspaper interview until his agent called to remind him. Ron asked about the procedure, but Chris didn't let on about too much discomfort. The reporter, Joe Augeri, had spoken to Ron a few nights earlier about Chris' story. *The Day* had always treated Chris well. The arts writer, Rick Koster, wrote a detailed piece about Chris' monster books, which Debbie had framed on a wall above the couch in the family room. *The Day* was a respected newspaper, earning several journalism awards both regionally and nationally. Augeri wrote columns in the sports section. When he heard about Chris' story, he nearly ran to get the column into the paper. Ron seemed impressed with his sincerity and interest.

Chris was appreciative of the phone interview. At least something took his mind off the chills and hot flashes. During the 30-minute conversation, Chris took his blanket on and off four times, and removed his sweatshirt twice. He was, however, careful about sounding upbeat, not uncomfortable.

Augeri asked good questions, well beyond the, "so how does it feel?" drivel heard so often from television sideline reporters. He couldn't get over the effect football had on Chris' life. He also felt a kinship of sorts. Augeri had written several columns hammering the high school administration and the town of East Lyme for the treatment of Dick North, Chris' high school coach, who was relieved of his duties as athletic director a few years earlier and died not long after.

"Will this be in the paper soon?" Chirs asked.

"If we could run a special edition right now, this afternoon, we would," Augeri said. "I mean, you couldn't make this stuff up."

The conversation ended pleasantly. Augeri asked if he could call periodically to monitor Chris' progress and maybe even come out to Chicago with him. Chris said he'd have to run it by Ron Laitsch.

He hung up the phone and went to sleep for a while, awakening when Debbie came home. He told her to read the paper in the morning and went back to sleep again, happy that he hadn't been nauseous all afternoon.

CHAPTER EIGHTEEN

Joe Augeri's story appeared in *The Day* the following morning. Chris had no idea that news of the piece had also made the radio. Frank Carafano's radio show on Q-105 in New London was awash in Chris' story. Carafano had the highest ratings of any morning show in eastern Connecticut, meaning that anybody who didn't read the newspaper likely discovered the Schildt story from the radio. In the process, Chris was becoming an unwitting celebrity.

Debbie left the house with a huge grin. This business of football and unwavering exercise left her a bit disillusioned at times. But it all seemed to make more sense once she saw it in print. That morning, Debbie's desk at work was littered with copies of *The Day* when she arrived. Debbie was prominent in the column, too, because of her patience and support. She didn't discuss Chris' past health problems much at work, except to the few with whom Debbie felt close. When some of the details made the newspaper, her co-workers were simultaneously thrilled and sympathetic. She called Chris around noon, happy to find that he was feeling better.

Chris had just finished talking to Debbie when he felt a nap was in order. He had just discovered the most comfortable position on the couch, legs still elevated, when the phone rang.

"At least they didn't wait till I was comfortable," Chris mumbled to himself.

He couldn't get off the couch very quickly. The machine picked up before Chris could get to the phone.

"Pick up. I know you're there," a voice said. It was Ron Laitsch.

"You must have ESP," Chris replied, after reaching the phone.

"I have ESPN., too," Ron said.

"I assume you saw the story online?"

"My God," Ron answered, "that couldn't have worked out better."

Ron's timing for a little publicity helped Chris forget about the chills and hot flashes. Like Debbie, seeing the story in print seemed to put everything into perspective. It took a few more days for Chris to begin exercising again. While his back was feeling better, he was feeling listless. Chris hadn't been eating much, mostly because he was only renting the food he ate. Inevitably, he would be nauseous after every meal.

Five days later, Chris decided he would go for a short run. He could always walk home if he didn't feel well. He wore a gray Bears' sweatshirt with the blue and orange logo above the words "Property of the Chicago Bears." He was feeling pretty good as he went up Beacon Hill to Vauxhall Street Extension. Chris was running with traffic. Cars passed as they always did, and Chris paid little attention to them, until a green Honda Accord appeared. The driver zipped past him, and then stopped the car. Chris thought that the guy might need directions. The driver waited for him to jog alongside the car. He rolled down the passenger's side window. Chris leaned over so he could look at the man behind the wheel. He was wearing a blue fleece jacket with what must have been his company's logo, and had on a baseball cap advertising some kind of tire a company.

"Go Bears!" the stranger yelled.

Chris didn't know what to say in reply.

"Uh…thanks," Chris finally said hesitantly. It wasn't often Chris didn't have a snappy comeback.

The driver rolled up the window, pumped his fist one last

time and drove on. Chris resumed his jog. He remembered that Augeri's column ran with a picture of Chris that Ron's agency had supplied.

Chris continued down Vauxhall for a while before turning around to reverse his course. He made the left on Grabner, which becomes Beacon Hill. He was running with his head down, unaware that a woman, who lived in one of the houses on Beacon, was standing at the curb. She was bringing her trash can back into the garage after the Friday pickup. He looked up and saw the woman smiling.

"Rah-kee! Rah-kee!" she cheered loudly.

Chris grinned at the reference to fictional character Rocky Balboa. What Chris didn't know was that another local radio station, after reporting his story, had dedicated the song "Eye of the Tiger" to him, from the motion picture, *Rocky III.*

"Thanks," Chris said. "Getting a little tired, though."

"Tired? You can do it!" she hollered. "We're all behind you!"

Just a few months ago, this was the same guy who would walk around wearing a disgusted expression that screamed, "Please don't bother me." He had no idea anybody in the Village knew who he was or what he did. Chris was the guy who was home all the time while Debbie went off to work. There were plenty of folks in the Village that thought he was just a lay-about, who was supported by his wife. They didn't realize that Chris was a writer, and home *was* his place of business.

By the time Chris reached the house, Debbie had returned home from work. She came flying through the door. Someone at work told her about Chris' mention on not one, but three radio stations, which she blurted out to him inside of 30 seconds upon seeing him.

"Really?" Chris said casually.

Debbie nodded her head excitedly. This was the first time that Debbie understood the scope of what was about to happen. It sounded a bit surreal at first--your husband having the chance to spend some time with an NFL team at the age of 45 and with a history of a fractured spine. The positive reaction all day, the newspaper article, radio stations and her patients at work who knew her, drew a clearer picture. Debbie even heard about the stranger in the Honda and the *Rocky* song dedication. On it went for the next week. People stopped Chris all over town. *If* only "Mike," from 30 years ago, could have been around to witness such a glorious return, especially after all that he had been through. The boy who had nearly died alone in a hospital from pneumonia, the boy no one would even talk to at school or even remembered, was about to become a legend. At Waterford's Crystal Mall, people pointed a finger at Chris and stared. Every once in a while he would hear, "Give 'em hell!" from a shopper, men and women alike. He even received a letter from the town's first selectman, Paul Eccard, telling him how very proud Waterford was of him. Chris couldn't help but contrast Waterford's support against the disdain he got from East Lyme 30 years ago.

The notoriety was beyond anything he'd imagined. Chris decided to drive to the radio station to thank Frank Carafano's, then later to *The Day* to see Augeri in person. Carafano wasn't at the Q-105 studio. Augeri wasn't around, either, but Chris left a message on his voicemail, inviting him to dinner at a place of Joe's choice. For Augeri, the choice was easy. He was a regular at Tony D's, New London's newest and best restaurant. It was a mixture of a chop house and upscale Italian. Tony "D" stood for proprietor Tony D'Angelo, one of the city's legendary characters. Tony was colorful, quotable and Ajax tough. He opened the restaurant in the downtown area a few years earlier, helping revitalize a once charming part of a historical whaling city. Augeri returned the call and suggested Tony's. He and his wife, Karin, would go with Debbie and Chris that Friday night. Chris insisted on paying the check.

Reservations weren't easy on a Friday at Tony's, but Augeri was becoming a fixture there, like Norm Peterson from the television show, *Cheers*. Chris and Debbie hadn't been there in a while. They were a bit stunned at the crowd in the dining room.

Augeri and his wife were late so Chris and Debbie went to the lounge for a drink, even though Chris didn't drink anything but cranberry juice. It was a horseshoe bar with perfectly polished brass, and it was full. So were the tables in the lounge. Debbie ordered a white zinfandel, while Chris studied the pictures that adorned Tony's walls. They included Bobby Darin, Sinatra, Secretariat and Tony's father, Sal. Augeri and his wife arrived and got the "lovers' booth," the most intimate one, tucked away in a corner. The booths were made of fine leather. There were several of them surrounding tables in the middle of the room. Intimate lighting reflected off the china and silverware that glistened. Joe didn't need a menu opting for the calamari, the appetizer specialty, with Caesar salad, veal chop and tiramisu for dessert.

Between Joe, Chris and the wives, there was a lot of laughter at the table, which is why Debbie thought that people were staring. When Chris stood up to use the restroom, though, she figured it out. A man and his wife approached Chris excitedly and asked him for his autograph. He signed it, with a sense of humility. Debbie turned to Joe Augeri.

"He gets that a lot these days," she said.

Augeri chuckled. "Pretty soon, they'll be walking up to Phil

Simms and saying 'hey, aren't you Chris Schildt?'"

Augeri took a swig of the cabernet waiting for the celebrity to return to the table. After the meal, a waitress came over to Chris, telling him that dinner was on Tony. Dinner at Tony D's was, as usual, an event. Tony had long since removed the menus from the table, preferring to let his four guests sample what felt like the entire right side of the menu. "Tony's Tomatoes," scallops, calamari, two chicken dishes, pasta, veal and three different desserts were responsible for making dinner last longer than some college football games.

When dinner ended and Tony's floor show had moved on to another table, Chris
had an idea.

"Let's go to Mohegan," he said.

"Let's," the others said in agreement.

Mohegan is the Mohegan Sun Casino, which has been on its way to becoming the state's No. 1 entertainment destination. The Sun had just added a second casino, the Casino of the Sky, which had a chic mall and oft-mentioned waterfall attached. The casino was established in the mid 90s with the Casino of the Earth, which had less frills and more gaming area.

The Sky Casino has a 10,000-seat arena attached, attracting the state's best concerts, championship boxing, and even rumblings of arena football and a Women's National Basketball Association franchise one day. Connecticut had become the nation's heartbeat for the women's game ever since UConn won its first national championship in 1995. Many of the nation's top musical acts were bypassing the Hartford Civic Center in favor of the Sun, which was building a snazzy new hotel on the property.

The mall surrounding the arena has two levels. Restaurants and bars dot the top floor, everything from barbeque to Michael

Jordan's Steakhouse, while trendy stores occupy the bottom, bisected by The Waterfall, the casino's top meeting place. The Sun's easy access from the highway made it both glitzy and convenient, a combination that added to the popularity.

Chris and Joe headed for the race book in the older casino to check out a few baseball scores, while Debbie and Karin went to the slots. They could make $20 last for hours on the 25-cent video poker machines.

CHAPTER NINETEEN

The first sunset Chris Schildt recalls from his childhood came in the company of two prostitutes. He met them when he was seven years old, alone in a bar where his father left him. That's the way life used to be for him in Florida, especially when he was under his father's watch. Chris was never exactly sure what his father was doing when he left him alone. Nothing was ever mentioned to his mother. That would only cause more fighting in the house, and there was enough of that. And Chris never accepted the money his father offered him to keep quiet. His father truly wasn't a bad person, Chris thought. No boy likes to think bad about his own dad. Chris was certain that he was just another emotional casualty of World War II , abused as a prisoner of war.

Chris always thought that it was the time his dad spent as a P.O.W. that accounted for alcoholism and his treatment of his own family. There was even one occasion when his father, drunk as usual, made Chris eat a bowl of cereal that was infested with cockroaches. Chris could feel them crawling in his mouth as he chewed. His dad had a rather twisted policy about wasting food, even if the food was bad. In the prison camps during the war, there was little food to eat. When Chris begged his father to allow him to spit out the cereal, his dad got angry at him. He ordered Chris to finish every last bite. When he became nauseous, his father punished him with a spanking. Even as an adult, Chris would check his food for bugs before eating.

His father still lived in East Lyme, but remained a stranger to his six children. As Chris would discover in early February, his dad's life rested somewhere at the bottom of a bottle, especially after Chris' mother was placed in a nursing home because of Alzheimer's disease.

More than a week had passed since the first spinal injection. Chris was slowly feeling better. Chris had been thinking about his father lately, wondering if a visit would be worthwhile. There had always been a certain emotional distance between them, but like so many fathers and sons, when they couldn't communicate about anything else, there was always sports. But Jim Schildt had always been a Colts' fan. He really didn't give a damn about the Chicago Bears or any other team.

Chris was consumed by football again. So much so that he forgot his cell phone during a trip to New London. He owed Ron a return phone call for some Bears business, and stopped to use a pay phone at Hughie's, a local restaurant and New London landmark. Hughie's had, to the delight of city residents, reopened two months earlier in a different section of the city than the old place. The old Hughie's, at the end of Howard Street, near the old Naval Undersea Warfare Center, was recently razed in the name of progress. A major drug company had become the centerpiece of the city's redevelopment, buying property to build a research center near the Thames River. Hughie's happened to be in the way. Its owner, Hughie Devlin, was compensated quite well for his life's business. He was the son of former professional boxer, Hughie Devlin Sr. That meant the walls of the bar area in the old Hughie's were their own unofficial Boxing Hall of Fame and history lesson. Old photos and news clippings of legendary fights at Madison Square Garden provided the scenery, along with photos of Hughie Jr. with sports personalities.

Hughie, a lifelong friend of Tony from Tony D's, was another inimitable character that gave New London its fighting spirit.

When the old Hughie's closed in August of 2000, patrons thought it would be closed forever. Hence, they took silverware, menus, dishes, bowls and glasses as souvenirs. Hughie had to hit a wholesale club to buy enough plates, forks and glasses to survive the final weekend.

Hughie's was known for two things: sports arguments at the bar and garlic. The "Love Salad," a collage of lettuce, tomatoes, salami, cheese, grated cheese, oil, vinegar and garlic, was the signature dish. It came in a classic wooden bowl and wouldn't leave you for several days. Hughie would never divulge the recipe. The dish had such pungent garlic aroma and taste that all New Londoners could tell when someone had eaten one. The waft of garlic would arrive in places ten minutes before the patron did.

Hughie decided that retirement wasn't the same as spending his days at the restaurant where he would tell old stories, shake hands and buy drinks, as the unofficial mayor and greeter of New London. And so, a little more than a year after the old Hughie's closed, the new one opened on Bank Street, just down the road from *The Day* newspaper. It had a bigger bar and restaurant area. Love Salads and garlic had made their triumphant return.

Chris hadn't been inside the old Hughie's in a while. He couldn't believe the snazzy new one. It had much better lighting and atmosphere. He wasn't interested in eating, even though the Love Salad, shrimp scampi and garlic bread sounded appetizing. All he wanted to do was make a phone call from the pay phone and go home.

He walked toward the phone, his mind occupied by a thousand different things, when Chris happened to see his father. Jim Schildt was at the bar, nursing what looked like a seven and seven. He could tell from his father's glassy eyes that it wasn't his first of the day, and likely not his last. Jim was sitting on the last barstool on the right side of the bar, under the television, wearing an Army baseball cap. There was no way Chris could avoid saying hello.

He nudged the guy sitting next to his father, a forty-something redhead with a red beard, speckled with a touch of gray. He was wearing a green and gold New London Whalers sweatshirt, trumpeting the local high school team. New London guys, once prone to crow about the school's excellence in football, boys' basketball and baseball, were beginning to lament where all the talent had gone. It had been a tough few years athletically at what had once been the only high school for miles, but if there was a place in town someone would still wear the colors, it was Hughie's. Chris whispered to the man that he was trying to surprise his father. The man nodded his head, smiled, then moved graciously to the left. Chris slid in and ordered a cranberry juice.

"Cranberry juice?" Jim Schildt said. "Christ's sake. Sure you can handle just one?" Jim grinned as he said it, and returned to his drink.

Chris figured his dad was just trying to break the ice. Still, no words were spoken for a good five minutes. Chris had spent the day of his spinal injections lamenting how long it took for a couple of minutes to pass. This five-minute bout with silence felt much longer.

"So, Mr. Cranberry Juice, you come here often?" Jim asked. He was trying to be friendly.

Chris sat silent. He realized that his father had no idea that he was talking to his own son.

"That stuff's no good for you," Jim said raising his glass, "but it doesn't affect your hearing."

"Hearing?" Chris looked at him, confused.

"Forget it," his father answered.

"I don't come here much," Chris said, figuring he should keep the conversation moving.

Jim embarked on his life story, or a least his version of it. Chris looked at him, tuning out the words, knowing that Jim thought he was talking to a complete stranger. Chris could have interrupted him a number of times to explain who he was, but figured it was pointless.

Then he heard his father say, "I got a couple kids, but I don't see them much."

Six, in his words, had become "a couple."

Chris took the last swig of his cranberry juice. He threw two twenty dollar bills down on the counter and told the bartender to make certain that Jim drove home in a cab. He would have tried to ask his father to go home with him, but he knew better. Pulling Jim Schildt out of a bar meant a fist fight, and Chris had had enough of that when he was a kid.

He walked outside with his head down. It felt like old times, sitting in a bar, wondering when his father would return or decide to head for home. He didn't turn the radio on during the ride home. Chris thought about how much his own boys meant to him, feeling proud about being a good father.

Chris with Russ Reiderer, the Bears' physical development coordinator

CHAPTER TWENTY

Selectman Paul Eccard spent the weekend showing a few relatives from out of state the beauty of his town. Eccard had been the assistant director of the town's park and recreation department for 25 years before getting elected in 1999. He was born in Waterford, educated there, and tells his friends, quite proudly, he will die there.

Eccard's relatives, who had never been to the town, couldn't believe a shoreline community of 19,000 could offer so much to its residents. Paul, who spent an entire Sunday in February driving them to the town's various sites, was the unofficial town historian, as well as selectman.

Their conversation flowed like the scenery. Waterford, an agricultural and fishing town of 7,000 before World War II, had nearly tripled in size since. It now had its own schools and sense of community. Waterford residents used to go to high school in New London, at either Bulkeley or Chapman Tech, before Waterford High School was built after the war.

Eccard was enjoying every mile of their drive through town. He could narrate about the place he loved with an interactive, captive audience of three cousins in the backseat. Waterford is nothing, if not picturesque, particularly through its water views. The town's beaches provided the serenity of being near water with a view that couldn't help but raise real estate prices.

Eccard's tour began near his house in Quaker Hill, a section of northeast Waterford. They drove past Mamacoke Island, which is surrounded by the Thames River, for a peek at the wildlife preserve. From there, they went west up route 85 to the town's rural section, passing Waterford Speedbowl, where auto racing enlivens Saturday nights in the summer with the sounds of revving engines. Few towns in Connecticut could offer such peaceful farm country and a breathtaking shoreline.

Eccard was quick to get back to the beach for the sunset because it had to be seen in two places: on Niantic River Road near the businesses along route 156, and at Stenger Farm Park, across from Clark Lane School. Stenger Farm Park was first. Eccard stopped the car and told his cousins to look west where the Oswegatchie Hills rolled on right into the horizon. Oswegatchie was the northern section of town that bordered East Lyme, where Chris once lived and went to high school. The day ended for the tour at Mago Point off Niantic River Road, where the sun was just about invisible, sliding down beyond the water. Mago Point offered a view of both the Thames River to the right and Long Island Sound to the left. Water could be seen endlessly, looking as if it met with the sky in the distance.

"This town is full of secrets and surprises," Eccard said to his family as he drove.

He told them two of the town's most famous stories about playwright Eugene O'Neill and former president Woodrow Wilson. The Eugene O'Neill Theater is in Waterford because O'Neill spent many years there. He actually swam at Waterford Beach when he was younger. Woodrow Wilson's sister used to spend summers in Oswegatchie, inviting her brother to the house for an occasional retreat. Little did Paul Eccard realize that the town was about to add another celebrity to their small, but distinguished list – a penniless kid from the South by the name of Christopher Mike Schildt.

Eccard arrived at town hall at 8 a.m. the next morning. His office offered a view of traffic that zipped back and forth on 156, as well as Waterford High School in the distance. Eccard played football at Waterford High in the early 60s. Every time he saw the lights illuminated for a Friday night game, he went over to watch a few quarters. The previous season, Waterford made the state playoffs for the first time in school history, a season in which Eccard took much delight.

There were times when he could close his eyes and picture his old coach, Ralph Kehoe, yelling, "Gentlemen!" when he wanted their attention. He remembered the old pre-game rituals, where Kehoe would blast patriotic music to inspire his players. Every now and then, when all was quiet, Paul Eccard's could hear the music even after all these years.

Eccard's office walls were covered with history. There was a copy of the Gettysburg Address over his spacious, oak desk, which was covered with folders and papers. He was something of a Civil War buff. His great, great, great grandfather, Giddeon Eccard, had fought in the battle of Gettysburg.

Lincoln's words, which Eccard said reminded him of how he's supposed to act while in office, were to the right of a television set bracketed to the wall, and to the left of the Waterford Town Seal featuring the words, "Agriculture, Industry, Prosperity, Waterford, 1801." An artist's drawing of the Harkness Mansion, which dominates the state park, sat on the wall behind him.

Across the room, there was a map of Waterford hanging by a rectangular window. Anyone could easily point anywhere on that map, and Eccard could identify the place and why it was significant to the town and its history.

As he sipped his coffee, Paul opened the newspaper. On the front page of the sports section, Eccard came upon the Augeri story about Chris. He slowly stood up, as he stared at the paper with a sense of amazement. Paul quickly strolled over to the various departments in town hall, to see if anyone else read it.

They all had. A dusty town in Texas had their Jim Morris, "The Rookie," and baseball. Now, Waterford had Christopher Mike Schildt and football. Paul immediately wrote Chris a quick note, telling him how proud the town was of his impending trip to the Bears' camp, ending it with, "Give 'em hell!" Augeri's column casually reminded Paul of the novel *Paper Lion*. It was one of his favorite books. Eccard read it at Lawrence and Memorial Hospital many years ago while he recovered from a broken right clavicle, sustained playing high school football.

Chris was overwhelmed by the note. The day he received it, he went to town hall to see if he could speak with Eccard for a minute. Joan Barnes, Eccard's assistant dating back to their days at the park and recreation department, managed to carve out a few minutes for them. They visited for longer than that.

CHAPTER TWENTY-ONE

The plan was executed flawlessly. Chris would fly from T.F. Green in Providence to Midway Airport in Chicago. Ron Laitsch, still a bit fretful about flying, would take a rental car from Atlanta to Chicago and meet Chris at baggage claim. So, a little after noon on a sunny day in late April with enough of a chill to be football weather, Chris Schildt spotted his agent walking toward him wearing a reassuring smile. It was one day before the improbable, if not a glorious end to Chris' football career, and the realization of a dream.

Ron drove his client to a hotel several miles away from Midway, closer to Lake Forest, site of the Bears' training facility. They'd spent the night in a hotel before Chris would report early the next day to Chicago Bears' mini-camp, the prelude to preseason camp four months later, signaling the start of the season. Chris would be there in Lake Forest on the Bears premises with Ron at his side on the following day.

Chris wasn't saying much. It was a subdued ride from the airport. He took a nap not long after they arrived at the hotel while Ron went to the exercise room. They promised to meet for dinner a few hours later.

Ron could sense the anxiousness in Chris' face. Sure, there was excitement, but also a sense of doubt. Chris couldn't help but wonder how he'd be treated as an outsider. Ron tried to take his mind off football at dinner in the hotel restaurant.

"So when are you going to write again?" Ron asked.

Chris looked startled. No one had really asked him about writing much in the last few months. The *Phantom of the Opera* project was either on hold or in the wastepaper basket.

Ron Laitsch

"I've got something up my sleeve," Chris replied with a wry grin. The only thing Chris had up his sleeve was his elbow. He had nothing planned, but the answer sounded good at the time.

"Look, you're going to be fine out there," Ron said. "I mean, look at the shape you're in. Think about how screwed you'd be if you hadn't lost 40 pounds."

Chris said nothing. Instead, he smiled and nodded his head. He looked down at his plate and stabbed a piece of salmon. He was still into high protein, low carbohydrate eating. Chris wondered if he should have ordered pasta since the extra carbohydrates would provide more energy, but decided to stick with the plan that got him there.

That night, Chris didn't sleep much. It was the fear of the unknown, he decided. The next morning, they awoke early and headed to the facility around 7 a.m. They were driving for maybe 30 minutes when Ron spotted their destination at the end of the long access road called Football Drive. They arrived at the security gate and were met by an official-looking guard. Ron gave security their names.

"Oh, yeah!" the man said. Then he smiled at Chris. It was a broad smile. "Gentlemen, welcome to the Chicago Bears."

Chris could feel a tingle up his spine where there had been nothing but pain. He swore he could hear the drums playing in the band, part of the inspiring pre-game symphony. Only this pre-game had lasted 30 years. Images of Gayle Sayers, Butkus and the rest flashed through his thoughts, mixed with the sound of coaches blowing their whistles and grunting players in the distant training fields at Halas Hall.

The guard told Ron where to park. As they drove past the security gate, Ron stopped the car, 20 feet away.

"Well, this is it. Are you ready?" Ron asked.

"No," he replied solemnly, "but Mike is."

They both smiled. Now there was nothing left to do but to drive on to Halas Hall. A certain magic rings in the name Halas Hall. It sounded like a wing of the Hall of Fame. George Halas, who would become among the most influential people in the history of the sport, founded the Bears in the 1920s and coached them for 40 years. The National Football Conference champion wins the George Halas Trophy every year.

George Halas, who was a native of Chicago, was a letterman in three sports at the University of Illinois. After college, he joined the Navy. He played for the New York Yankees after his tour of duty until a hip injury ended his baseball career. As a coach for the Chicago Bears, Halas held three NFL records. His record of 324 coaching victories remained until 1994 when it was broken by Don Shula of the Miami Dolphins. George Halas had led the Bears to six world championships. The team was now under the management Ted Phillips, president and CEO, and Jerry Angelo, the team's general manager.

Ted Phillips was born in Onieda, New York, and had grown up in Nashua, New Hampshire. He had earned a master's degree in marketing and management from the Kellogg Graduate School at Northwestern University. Prior to joining the Chicago Bears, Ted Phillips had worked as an auditor and tax accountant with the firm of Ernst & Whinney between the years of 1979 to 1983. He had originally joined the Bears as the team's comptroller in 1983. By 1999, he had been appointed as the team's' executive officer focusing his efforts on restoring respectability to the team's proud tradition.

Jerry Angelo, after spending 14 years overseeing the Tampa Bay Buccaneers' scouting department as the director of Player Personnel, was given control of the Bears' football operations on June 12, 2001. In Tampa, he helped turn a team that averaged fewer than five wins a season in its first 21 years into a permanent playoff contender. Prior to the Buccaneers, Jerry had spent five seasons with the New York Giants as a regional scout, which included their Super Bowl XXI season.

Together, Ted Phillips and Tony Angelo had formed a symphony of courage and dignity cast in bronze. There's no doubt that George Halas would have been damned proud of them.

Chris walked into the main hall and was overcome by a portrait of Halas, to the left of the entrance. The rendering was made of tile, showing him in his old football uniform from college, with closely-cropped hair, hands on hips and loose-fitting pants. Chris' eyes then saw a trophy case, dominated by a painting, a collage of Bears' history. He wasn't saying a word. Chris just stared in wonder until his jaw dropped at the site of the Vince Lombardi Trophy commemorating the Bears' Super Bowl championship, won in January, 1986. Chris noticed how the light shining on the trophy illuminated it perfectly, brighter than everything else in the entrance hall. He shook his head, unable to fathom where he was standing. Ron finally tugged at his left arm, guiding him in the direction of the front desk.

"Can I help you?" a friendly voice asked. It was the receptionist.

Chris, once again, wasn't talking. His eyes gazed at the ring of NFL helmets that
hung over the desk in a circle. It was like Disney World, but for men. Ron gave the woman their names.

"We know exactly who you are," she said, with the same comforting smile as
the security guy. "Chris, welcome to the Bears."

Still, Chris could hardly speak. All he could do was smile and nod his head appreciatively with a sense of humility.

They turned around to see Scott Hagel running down a flight of stairs that led to the office of upper management. Ron had talked to Hagel on the phone several times. He was expecting an older man. Iinstead, Hagel looked to be no older than 20 or so, wearing khaki pants, a Bears' sweatshirt and a Bears' cap. It looked as though he had removed his college cap and gown only a few days earlier. But looks *can* be deceiving. In reality, Scott Hagel was one of the finest in his field in the NFL.

Chris began to wonder if it was team policy to look reassuring. Hagel was unwaveringly friendly, adding his welcome. Chris should have been the honored one in the presence of an NFL team, yet he was made to feel as though everyone was there to greet him.

"Okay. The first thing we do is get you to the equipment room," Hagel said,
leading them down the hall.

The equipment room is Tony Medlin's province. He is a Bears' fixture, the equipment manager since 1987, able to narrate, quite jovially, about every nut, bolt and screw that holds NFL equipment together, as well as provide a textbook's history, all the way to the days when the shoulder pads and helmets were leather.

Hagel told Ron and Chris about Tony's legend in the organization, mentioning the Whitney Zimmerman Award as the league's top equipment man in 2000, and his loyalty to the community through charity work. Hagel just finished talking about Tony's brother, Ron, the Atlanta Falcons' equipment manager, as the three men entered the room. Medlin and Chris would become fast friends. Tony was that way with everyone. He shook Chris' hand, and then Ron's. He gave them a brief tour of the room before looking at

Scott Hagel of the Bears

Chris and saying, "I know exactly what size you are."

"Don't you need to take a measurement?" Chris asked, half smiling.

"I'm not a tailor," Medlin cracked.

Medlin surveyed Chris for another few seconds, and said, "Size 'L' pants, size 'L' T-shirt."

Chris had a hard time believing he wasn't an 'XL' anything anymore. That's what happens when you go from the 220s to south of 180.

"I really think I'm an XL," Chris said hesitantly, almost apologetically out of respect for Medlin.

"Okay, but it's going to look like a dress," Medlin said.

Medlin was correct.

Next, it was on to the shoulder pads. Medlin, a few inches shorter than Chris, found a pair and placed them over Chris' head. They're made of industrial strength plastic now with product logos splashed on them, like a race car. Medlin fit them snugly over Chris' gray T-shirt.

"How is this plastic stuff supposed to protect a guy? You mean they're not made of leather?" Chris asked.

"Boy, you have been away from the game a while," Tony Medlin chuckled, shaking his head.

Shoulder pads were leather at East Lyme in 1972. Medlin took a short walk to the other side of the room to find Chris a dark navy Bears' helmet, with the orange "C" logo. There wasn't a more recognizable symbol in the NFL.

"Do you know how to put one of these on?" Medlin asked.

Chris scored big points here. He slid his index fingers through the holes, moved his thumbs underneath to stretch it, and pulled it over his head.

"Like riding a bicycle," Chris said.

"Atta boy!" Medlin seemed impressed. "So you *do* know

Chris with Bears' equipment manager, Tony Medlin

what you're doing. Did they do that with leather helmets, too?"

Chris laughed. Then he told Medlin about the old helmets he remembered with canvas straps.

Medlin sat Chris in a chair and inserted a needle into the back of the helmet. To Chris, this was strange. A needle for a helmet? He had felt enough of those in his spine.

"Are you going to inflate my head?" Chris asked.

Medlin giggled. Chris could feel the helmet inflate, making it fit more comfortably. It was also safer in the event of a blow to the head.

Now it was time for Chris' pants, white with navy and orange stripes down each side. This was another new experience. Chris was used to loose-fitting uniform bottoms with laces. It's almost as though society had run a reverse: Thirty years later, tight football pants and baggy jeans had replaced baggy football pants and the tight jeans of the 1970s.

Chris attempted to buckle the pants. They were too tight.

"Buckle them, or I'll buckle them for you," Tony Medlin said.

Chris gave one last tug and it worked. He couldn't believe the snugness or how that's the way they were supposed to fit.

Tony walked over with the final piece, the navy uniform top. Chris would wear No. 80. It was short-sleeved. The "80"came in white, outlined in orange. There were numbers on the outside of each shoulder also white outlined in orange, on top of three, circular orange stripes, outlined in white.

Medlin stretched two pieces of two-sided carpet tape and applied them to the uniform, forming an adhesive. And there he was, looking like a Chicago Bear. Too bad Chris didn't have much time to savor it.

"Okay. Take it all off," Tony Medlin said. "I'll have it all ready in a locker."

Before Chris peeled off the layers, he posed for a picture with Ron who had been soaking in the scenery. This was a big day for him, too. Chris leaned over to Ron who was wearing a light, royal blue jacket with a green stripe. Ron held up the helmet with a wide smile.

Scott Hagel had returned to give the two of them a tour of the facility.

First, there was the media room. Not where the sportswriters filed their stories, but where the players could study film. Any play from any game and any team. Slow it down. Speed it up. There was a battalion of television screens, computers, filming equipment and remote controls. Chris didn't know which button he would have wanted to push first.

The medical taping room was across the hallway. Elevated seats much like shoe-shine chairs, sat along a glass wall,

Chris and Ron

making ankle-taping easier. A training table with all the equipment in the standard first-aid kit was about five feet away, across from the chairs. In front of the doorway lay two medicine balls – blue and green to match Ron's jacket – along with an exercise bike underneath a row of cabinets. A television monitor was bracketed from the ceiling, hanging between the elevated chairs and the doorway.

Hagel took Chris and Ron outside to walk the field. It was manicured in emerald green, much as you'd expect at Yankee Stadium in the summer. Goalposts sat at each end, in front of some woods, whose trees still didn't have many leaves. It looked a little like fall, without the foliage.

Players were scattered about. Nothing formal was happening. To Chris, if felt as if he had finally come home again.

CHAPTER TWENTY-TWO

Next, it was off to the physical development room to meet Russ Riederer, the Bears' physical coordinator. Riederer had been with the organization more than 10 years. He came from the Packers, where he was on the coaching staff with Dick Jauron, the Bears' current coach. Riederer was a hard working man in the organization, maintaining his diligence long after the season ended. He maintained strength and conditioning programs year-round, a vital practice even seeping down to high school programs.

Chris took one look at Riederer, and for a fleeting moment, thought that he saw Dick North, his old high school coach. Riederer, Midwestern tough, still had the linebacker's body from his days playing at Kansas State. He wore a goatee, which coach North never had, but his closely cropped hair and pensive demeanor brought Chris back to his high school days.

Hagel made the introductions. Riederer had a rugged voice, but exuded a sense of compassion, which made Chris a bit more at ease.

The physical development room was quite bright, punctuated by dozens of fluorescent lights and several windows set high along the walls, allowing daylight to enter. Below the windows, about halfway up each wall, the word Bears was written, alternating between blue and orange letters.

The room was awash in free weights, weight machines and cardiovascular equipment, a fitness center that would make an owner of the corner gym salivate.

Chris was wearing his white Bears' T-shirt and blue shorts when Riederer's first request came: to measure his body fat.

Chris' mind flashed back 40 pounds ago, wondering if he'd have made the meter tilt like a whacked out pinball machine. The physical coordinator stood behind Chris. Chris removed his shirt.

The body fat reading, at approximately 12 percent, barely registered with Riederer, whom Chris could see was suddenly wearing a sour expression. Riederer exhaled, as if alleviating some stress, and turned to Ron Laitsch.

"Are you sure he should be here?" Riederer asked.

Riederer had just seen the surgical scars on Chris' back. They nearly formed a "V" shape. The vertical 10-inch scar radiated pain. Another four-inch scar veered to the left in a "V" shape. Pain was part of the deal in Riederer's area of expertise, but even he had trouble imagining the circumstances behind the "V."

Chris put his shirt back on.

"We have a neurosurgeon's permission," Ron Laitsch said.

Riederer patted Chris on the shoulder and offered him a reassuring smile.

Chris' first assignment, from a stationary position with his knees bent, was to jump up on a platform five feet off the ground. Again, his mind darted to a few months ago, when walking to the end of the driveway felt like an Olympic event.

Chris did it, but nearly at the complete expense of his back. Never had he felt such pain. It was as if an ice pick didn't just get him once, but repeatedly. He grimaced. Ron Laitsch, standing in front of him, read the reaction. Riederer, who was "spotting" Chris, was standing behind him in case he fell. He never saw the expression of pain on Chris' face.

"How did that feel?" Riederer asked.

"No problems," Chris answered.

If only that was the truth.

Riederer asked him to do three sets of five jumps as fast as he could. Chris could no longer think of the pain, which was constant and unwavering. If he thought about it, he'd have been forced to stop. Instead, he thought about the smell of the locker room, the feel of a helmet tucked under the arm during the national anthem. This got him through. If Chris had ever been more proud of himself, or more proud of Mike, in this case, he couldn't remember the occasion.

Riederer than asked Chris to run up a flight of 20 stairs, ten times, as fast as he could, skipping no steps. Chris loved this one. It began with a "foot fire" at the bottom of the steps, a pre-game ritual for football players for years. A foot fire comes when players run in place, knees bent, feet hitting the ground quickly, as if on fire.

It felt like high school again. Oh, how he remembered that drill. Maybe that's why he zipped up and down the steps with a ballet dancer's balance.

"Awright!" Riederer said, perhaps a bit startled at Chris' composure. Ron
Laitsch could be seen grinning, too.

Chris took a short break before the next task on a running machine. It was a treadmill, on a permanent, 15-degree incline to compensate for the weight of a football player's equipment. The difference between it and a treadmill: when the runner stopped, it stopped.

"Let's see how fast you are," Riederer said.

At 5' 9," Chris was never big in high school, but compensated with decent speed.
Riederer clocked him at 10 mph first. Not bad for a 45-year-old epileptic with a spine fracture.

"What's the fastest anyone's ever run on that?" Ron asked.

"About 19 mph," Riederer replied.

"You wanna see what an old defensive back can do?" Chris asked, smiling. "Watch this!"

Chris got it up to just less than 13 mph, much to Riederer's delight. Ron, again, looked like the proud father.

The final stop for the morning was a drill especially for receivers and defensive backs. Chris was to jump and touch the pegs on an elongated gadget, measuring his vertical leap. It would give coaches an idea of the player's ability to reach for the ball.

Chris began with his arms over his head, as though signaling "touchdown," so Riederer could set the device's appropriate height.

Riederer had to readjust it several times. Jumping ability was never Chris' specialty, especially when landing meant even more back pain. Chris wasn't happy with his performance on the last drill, but left the physical development room satisfied. Hagel told him it wasn't every day that Russ Riederer unloaded an "awright!"

Hagel, meanwhile, brought along a friend, Bears' cornerback R.W. McQuarters. Chris not only knew of him, but was a little awestruck.

"I thought you'd like to meet another defensive back," Hagel said.

They shook hands and started gabbing about the sport.

"I was playing before you were born," Chris eventually said.

McQuarters just shook his head. "Nah – can't be."

"Oh yeah? What year were you born?" Chris asked.

"Seventy-four."

Chris raised his eyebrows and smiled. "My last year was '73."

"Damn. You're like my father's age," McQuarters said chuckling.

A few minutes before, they were strangers. Now it felt more like two football players. They talked about their desires to play offense in high school, and the injuries that had affected them both. Chris told him the story behind his fractured spine, the paralysis and the pneumonia. R.W. hung on every word. They lost track of time.

CHAPTER TWENTY-THREE

From the day Chris learned he was going to the Chicago Bears training camp, he harbored a thought he didn't share with anyone: What if the sizzle was better than the steak? He was wondering whether the days leading to camp would be more rewarding than the experience in Lake Forest, mindful that he didn't know anyone and no one knew him.

No matter the degree of optimism with which he tried to condition himself, his back, epilepsy and general doubts crept into his thoughts far too often. This is a professional football franchise with intense business to conduct over a few days. Who the hell had time for him?

Chris had his answer…everyone. The sizzle had been symphonic, yet the experience was every bit the dream for which he prayed.

He spotted Scott Hagel in a brisk walk coming the other way. Scott slapped hands passing McQuarters, and headed to Chris as if they were both late for something. Scott Hagel always appeared to be running somewhere in a hurry.

"There's someone special I want you to meet," Scott said.

Chris wasn't sure where he needed to be next, figuring Hagel had the correct itinerary.

Someone special? That could have been anyone here. This is a flagship franchise with historical figures who could have their own wing at the Hall of Fame, Chris thought. This is a team coming off a 13-win season with emerging players Chris knew about from watching their playoff game in January against the Eagles.

"Where to?" Chris wondered.

Hagel led Chris down the hallway and to the playing field. Chris hoped the first time he ever stepped on the field would be in full uniform, but then who had time to be picky?

"Is there anything you need?" Hagel asked when the men were en route.

Chris could see it was a sunny day outside, one of those occasions when the
weather fit the mood.

"You know, the fact that you asked me that with everything else you've got going on ... it's unbelievable to me," Chris answered.

"So that's a 'no?'"

"I might need you to pinch me," Chris joked. "Other than that ..."Hagel chuckled. Chris had a smile, too, when the doors opened, and he saw two young men in wheelchairs. Their names were Rob and Rocky. Suddenly, the man who had snappy comebacks for most occasions didn't know what to say.

In the wheelchair to the left was Rob Komosa, a teenaged quadriplegic, paralyzed from the neck down. In the wheelchair to the right was Rocky, paralyzed from the waist down. They were the Bears' adopted sons, who came from the greater Chicago area.

Chris, suddenly, had the same epiphany as Ron did, the day Ron saw Chris 40 pounds lighter in the coffee shop. Everything was self-explanatory. That's why no one had to tell Chris that Rob and Rocky were injured playing high school football.

Rob, a white kid with dirty blonde hair and blue eyes, was the son of Polish immigrants. He was covered from head to toe in Bears' paraphernalia. He had a portable respirator with him. He was smiling, always smiling. That's all he ever did, despite his circumstances. Rocky, an African-American youth, wore a black Bears' cap with the orange 'C' logo and a dark sweatsuit.

"Guys, this is Chris Schildt. He was paralyzed as a high school football player 30 years ago," Scott Hagel said.

Chris was so profoundly affected by meeting Rob and Rocky, that he hardly noticed Ted Washington standing there. Washington, a mountainous, 300-plus pound defensive lineman, had been clowning around with the Bears' adopted sons when Chris and Scott Hagel arrived. A stranger, like Chris, would have thought the two boys were Washington's sons.

"Now you're walking again?" Rocky asked.

All Chris could do was nod. He fought back tears with the same resolve as his workout routine from home. He knew the last thing the boys needed to see was someone feeling badly for them. Finally, he lifted his T-shirt and showed them the scars on his back.

Scott Hagel was mesmerized for a few moments, listening to Chris, Rocky and Rob talk. They were, in a way, kinsmen. There was commotion from some players at the other end of the field, but otherwise, it was eerily quiet with just the sound of three voices. There wasn't much wind whipping through the trees in the distance nor were the birds contributing much. Maybe they wanted to hear the conversation, too.

The boys and Chris talked about the loneliness of hospitals. It was almost bearable when your friends were there, but those times when you were alone with your thoughts...

"I was alone a lot," Chris told them.

They related their injuries, happening on plays seemingly every high school football player has experienced. Except that they experienced the wrong hit, the ill-fated fall, and the life that changed forever.

They each contracted pneumonia, mostly from the inability to move. Many spinal cord injury patients battle pneumonia for that reason, although Chris' case was severe. Chris told the kids about the Last Rights and the weight loss.

The boys hung on each other's every word, creating a support system in the middle of a field, under a blue sky, sharing the same real estate as a professional football team. It became even more evident to Chris that the Bears weren't merely different from the rest of the NFL because of their history. He began to recall the stories Ron told him about all the teams that either never returned phone calls or passed on the opportunity to at least give Chris at chance. And then he saw the Bears' commitment through the compassion of the organization by adopting the kids. Chris and Scott Hagel then headed back to the locker room. Not a word was said. No, all the words really necessary happened between Chris and the boys. A seminal moment in Chris' life had just taken place. He had spent the last 30 years bitter over what had happened on that high school playing field in East Lyme. That bitterness was quickly replaced with a sense of appreciation that he had actually been so fortunate. And, somewhere in heaven, God must have been smiling warmly and compassionately down on a tiny piece of earth in Lake Forest, Illinois. To see these two young boys in wheelchairs so happy to see a man who was once paralyzed wearing a football uniform again. Truly this was a miracle made possible with the help of the Chicago Bears.

Chris as a Bear

CHAPTER TWENTY-FOUR

The players were on the field for a while, leaving Chris in an empty locker room, where he sat by himself. Chris' uniform lay in a cubicle of sorts. Most of Chris' fondest memories from high school football came in the locker room. The room had a certain din, always the home office for some pervasive emotion: anticipation for the game, euphoria after victory, depression after a loss. The walls echoed with howls of happiness, lockers slamming, showers running, toilets flushing and, of course, coach North's voice.

East Lyme's locker room, nonetheless, was a homeless shelter compared to what the Bears offered. East Lyme had tile floors and lockers. Lake Forest had wall-to-wall carpet and each player's individual space, complete with a stall, maybe four feet wide, to hang clothes and keep personal items. The showers were at one end of the room. The walls were painted white with plenty of navy-blue-and-orange Bears' logos.

Tony Medlin's work, quite clearly, was meticulous. Each article Chris was about to wear was immaculately presented: jersey, pants, helmet, shoulder pads and cleats all custom fit from the day before. If Tony had to do that for each player, how could he have time to eat, sleep, or go home, Chris thought to himself.

It was hard for him not to think about the day he was injured. Everything was all *so* innocent. It was a day that failed to distinguish itself from any of the others. It was just a pass play Chris had seen dozens of times. And it would affect the rest of his life. Chris tried to spend 30 years not thinking about it, yet at times, even with police work and novel writing more pressing, he could think of nothing else.

The pants, white with blue and orange trim, would be the first clothing Chris would wear. The shoulder pads were still ridiculous to him. Plastic? No leather? It was still 50-50 in Chris' mind whether they'd really work all that well. One thing about his leather shoulder pads from high school: He could have gotten rolled by a snowplow and those shoulder pads would have remained unharmed.

The shoulder pads fit snugly under a gray Yale T-shirt, which he wore for Chris Jr. Then, he walked over to a mirror to see the work in progress. It would have been difficult for him not to feel a bit strange, although there's really no handbook on how to feel during a seminal moment in your life. Still, Chris had been in so many vibrant locker rooms. The silence here felt a bit eerie.

The jersey, No. 80, slid over the shoulder pads. Chris sat down in front of
his stall and was about to lace up the footwear when he looked up and saw Ron Laitsch standing over him. Chris realized he was zoning out a bit, failing to hear him walk in. Chris was sitting on a folding chair with his helmet next to him.

All those days Chris would stand outside coffee shops in New York and chuckle at how Ron's facial expression would never change. He was so stoic with his nose in the newspaper, rarely alarmed by even New York noise.

"A father couldn't be any prouder of his son than I am of you right now," Ron Laitsch said solemnly.

Chris nodded his head, as Ron put his right hand on Chris' shoulder.

"I guess I'll see you later," he said.

Ron Laitsch walked out and Chris was alone again. Or so he thought.

He buried his head in his hands and sobbed. Tears of joy, tears of sentiment. From a hospital bed, paralyzed and nearly dead from pneumonia, to Lake Forest, Ill., wearing a uniform again. Chris wiped his eyes and looked around. He was in East Lyme again, but just for a moment. The moment before a game. He saw all his old teammates. He saw Arnie Hull and Stan Jaskiewicz. He smelled it again. It was always a little musty. And he could feel the uniform. He heard lockers slamming. He didn't hear much chatter, because it was right before the game, a time when a locker room is as quiet as graveyard.

He was sitting at his locker, on a bench that stretched the entire row. His helmet was by his side.

Oh, the crunching sound those cleats made on the tile floor. Chris could hear the toilets flushing from the other side. He saw an ocean of maroon and white, players tending to their last little pre-game details.

Now he was back in Lake Forest, back in the silence. The room was empty again. Chris leaned over to lace up his shoes, good and tight as always. Left foot first, then the right. He reached for his helmet and thought he heard a voice.

"Hey! Mighty Mouse!" It was coach North calling his old nickname.

Chris shut his eyes and could hear Dick North more clearly.

Coach North, wearing a maroon East Lyme jacket and hat, was pacing, saying, "Big game today, men. They don't think we can beat them. But they don't know what we've been through all week. And they certainly don't know Viking warriors..."

Chris could feel a tingle down his spine.

Suddenly, he jerked his head, as if coming out of a sleep. Tony Medlin had come in the room. Chris never heard him.

"Shouldn't you be somewhere?" he asked.

"Sorry, I guess I was just visiting the past," Chris shrugged. Then he looked into Tony's eyes, and his smile slowly faded. "You probably think I just a foolish old man."

"Nah," Tony Medlin replied. "I just think God had a different plan for you 30 years ago. I think he decided to save you for the Bears."

Chris closed his eyes and nodded.

Tony Medlin patted him on the shoulder pad and left the locker room through one of the side doors, then back to the equipment room.

Chris could see the door ajar. It was sunny early afternoon with players hooting and whistles tooting in the distance. Chris put his index fingers through the holes of the helmet and pulled it down over his head. He proudly stood up, and then walked out the door of the locker room.

Great to be alive!

The Team and 72!

EPILOGUE

When Chris left Halas Hall for home there was no cheering crowd. No one asked him for his autograph. There were no multi-million-dollar endorsement offers. There was only a flight to catch for home. None of that truly mattered to him, though. Chris realized that he had been given something that most can only dream of…a second chance. And this is where his story should have ended, but it didn't.

In 1973, when Chris lay motionless in the hospital at the U.S. Sub Base, Dick North brought him his high school jersey, No. 72. North was virtually the only visitor Chris had, making the gesture all the more extraordinary, then all the more heartbreaking. When Chris was moved to the intensive care unit, the jersey was stolen from his room. Chris never recovered it. As many years as Chris wondered why the injury happened to him, he spent as much time lamenting the loss of his jersey, and the cruelty behind stealing it. What sort of an individual would have stolen something *so* very precious from a boy who was near to death?

Seven months after his return from the Bears, with a No. 80 jersey sitting proudly in the family room, Chris was contacted by Andy Dousis, East Lyme's football coach, about his missing jersey. Dousis, amid his second winning season in the last three years, and known
throughout eastern Connecticut as one of its coaching gentlemen, couldn't have been kinder. One week before East Lyme would conclude its season on Thanksgiving Day with a game against Waterford, Chris attended an East Lyme practice.

The season began for the Vikings on a warm September

night, producing seven wins and three losses. Practice was to begin a little after three.

There was the quintessential November chill, despite more sunny weather than usual. Most of the grass on the field had faded to brown. Most of the trees lost their leaves, naked for a cold winter ahead. Football coaches' anticipation for the upcoming season is as giddy in August as it is depressing in November, when the end is in sight.

Dousis gathered his team on what would be foul territory down the right field line of the baseball field, which sits adjacent to the football field. The team often practices there, saving the football field for games. The bleachers on the visitors' side of the football field and the home dugout aren't more than twenty feet apart, separated by the food stand and a fence. By the end of the season, Dousis still had sixty players on the roster, only four years removed from a season in which the Vikings had around 20 by Thanksgiving. East Lyme, known as a soccer town, was developing a solid football program. Dousis' team defeated Fitch of Groton, the five-time defending league champion, and Stonington, a team that would make the state playoffs, in 2002.

Dousis presented Chris with his No. 72 jersey in both home and away colors, as the players took to a knee, watching solemnly. The maroon from the days Chris played was a lighter shade. It has since grown darker, to what has become almost a plum color. The home jersey, darker maroon, sported a white No. 72, outlined in black. The road jersey, white background, has a maroon 72, also outlined in black.

The presentation was sacred to Chris. Dousis shook his hand, leading to wild applause from the players. There was some irony in that. Chris never forgot how he was shunned by the people wearing the uniform following the injury.

"Someone that I knew, 30 years ago, asked me to offer his sincerest appreciation," Chris said, addressing the team. "His name was Mike, and he too wore the uniform of a Viking. He's sorry for not being here with you today. He's gone to where every good player goes when his time on the field is over, to that place at the sidelines to be at his coach's side. Somewhere, I know Mike is with Dick North. He also asked me to tell you that you, as a team, are not as good they were years ago. You're better! And you've given back to him something that was taken from him, a jersey and camaraderie."

Then Chris, Debbie, Andy, and Andy's captains walked across the football field toward the school, to the sign that welcomes visitors to the field: the Dick North Memorial Field. Debbie took several photos, one is now displayed in the family room. They knelt under the memorial sign, holding the home and away jerseys. Indeed, Mike and Dick North were reunited again. And no one on the team wore "72" that year. That number was reserved for "Mighty Mouse," a penniless kid from the South.

THE END

THE BEARS: A HISTORY IN BRIEF

"Bear down, Chicago Bears, make every play clear the way to victory;

Bear down, Chicago Bears, put up a fight with a might so fearlessly.

We'll never forget the way you thrilled the nation with your T-formation.

Bear down, Chicago Bears, and let them know why you're wearing the crown.

You're the pride and joy of Illinois, Chicago Bears, bear down."

Chicago Bears Fight Son

1920s: George Halas founded pro football and the Decatur Staley's in 1920 and set membership at $100 per club. The Staley's posted a 10-1-2 record in that inaugural season as each player earned $1,900 for the season. The Bears won their first title the next season (1921) with a 9-1-1 mark and went on to post winning records in all but one season in the entire decade (1929: 4-9-2). The first major signing took place in 1925 when the Bears signed Red Grange to a contract. Halas then took Grange and the Bears on a coast-to-coast barnstorming tour in which the club played 16 games in nine weeks. The first game of that stretch was played before 36,000 at the team's home site, Wrigley Field.

1930s: Halas left the coaching ranks in 1930 and Ralph Jones let the club to a 24-10-7 record from 1930-32. The Bears won the 1932 championship before 11,198 fans at Chicago Stadium. The franchise lost $18,000 that season and Sternaman sold his half of the club to Halas. The 1933 season marked Halas' return to coaching and the beginning of the "modern" National Football League. The Bears beat the Giants 23-21 in the NFL's first championship game that year. The Bears advanced to the NFL title game twice more in the 30s, but fell to the Giants in 1934 and the Redskins in 1937.

1940s: The decade began with another NFL title as the Bears buried the Washington Redskins, 73-0, as ten different players scored while Chicago unveiled the T-formation. Halas left for war duties in the middle of the 1942 season. The team continued winning, but lost the title game in Washington, 14-6. Luke Johnsos and Hunk Anderson co-coached the wartime Bears the next three seasons. In 1943, the Bears beat Washington 41-21 at Wrigley Field in the NFL title game. Halas returned in 1946 and the Bears won the title again – defeating the Giants, 24-14, before a NFL-record crowd of 58,346 in the Polo Grounds.

1950s: The Bears began the decade with a title run, but lost to the Rams in the 1959 Western Division title game, 24-14. Paddy Driscoll replaced Halas as coach in 1956 and the Bears lost to the Giants in the NFL Championship game at Yankee Stadium. Halas returned for his final stint as head coach in 1958.

1960s: The Bears won their final title under Halas in 1963, beating the NY Giants, 14-10, at Wrigley Field. A new era was signaled in 1965 when the club drafted Dick Butkus and Gale Sayers in the first round of the college draft. Sayers set a NFL record with 22 TDs as a rookie, including six in a single game against the 49ers. Prior to the 1968 season, Halas retired from coaching after 40 seasons and a 324-151-31 record. Ed McCaskey was named team's vice-president and treasurer in 1067, a position he held for 17 years before being named chairman of the board in 1983 and eventually chairman emeritus in 1999. Ed spearheaded the club's civic activities for many years and attends NFL meetings. Among his many civic contributions on behalf of the Bears was guiding the Brian Piccolo Fund from its inception in 1970 to 1987, raising millions of dollars for cancer research.

1970s: The Bears played their final season in Wrigley Field in 1970 before moving to Soldier Field. In the same year, Halas was elected president of the NFC as the NFL and AFL merged. In 1974, Jim Finks joined the Bears as general manager. Finks named Jack Pardee, the first non-Bear in such a position, as head coach replacing Abe Gibron. In 1975, the Bears moved their training camp to Lake Forest after spending 31 years in Rensselaer, Indiana; and Walter Payton was the club's first-round draft choice. After a 14-year hiatus, the Bears returned to the playoffs in 1977, winning their final six games to finish 9-5. The Bears again made the playoffs in 1979 under head coach Neill Armstrong. Chicago lost in the opening round in both 1977 and 1979. The organization suffered a major loss at the end of the decade when team President George "Mugs" Halas, Jr. died at 54. Mugs joined the Bears front office in 1950, was named treasurer in 1953, and became president of the club in 1963.

1980s: Armstrong's tenure ended in 1982 and he was replaced by Dallas Cowboys' assistant Mike Ditka, a Bears tight end from 1961-66. In 1983, Jim Finks resigned and George Halas died at age 88. Michael McCaskey, the oldest son of Ed and Virginia McCaskey and the grandson of George Halas, became the third president in club history. McCaskey was a business school professor and operated a consulting company in Boston before joining the Bears. In his 15 seasons as club president, the Bears posted nine winning seasons, made three trips to the NFC title game and won Super Bow XX. McCaskey has served stints on the finance, long range planning, stadium, and NFL properties executive committees during his tenure. The Bears returned to the NFL elite in 1984. They advanced to the NFC Championship game (losing to San Francisco) and Walter Payton broke Jim Brown's all-time NFL rushing record. The loss in the '84 title game set the stage for the 1985 season in which the Bears posted shutouts in both playoff games before ripping the Patriots, 46-10, in the Super Bowl XX. The Bears won the NFC Central division each of the next three seasons, but could never get past the NFC title game. Payton's jersey was retired following the '87 season.

1990s: The Bears made playoff appearances in 1990 and 1991. The 1992 season was marked by the retirement of Mike Singletary, the end of the Mike Ditka era and Kevin Butler becoming the club's all-time scoring leader. Dave Wannstedt was named the 11th head coach in team history in 1993 and led the Bears to back-to-back winning seasons in 1994 and 1995. The uniform numbers of Dick Butkus (51) and Gale Sayers (40) were retired in 1994. The team moved into its new headquarters, Halas Hall at Conway Park, on March 3, 1997. The Bears became the first franchise in NFL history to win 600 games; number 600 was a 13-7 win over Tampa Bay at Soldier Field (11-23-97). On August 1, 1998, Mike Singletary became the 24th Bear inducted into the NFL Hall-of-Fame, the most of any franchise. Dick Jauron became the 12th head coach in Bears history on January 24, 1999. Two weeks later the Bears reshuffled the front office by naming Ted Phillips president and CEP, Michael McCaskey chairman of the board, and Ed McCaskey chairman emeritus. Chicago mourned the passing of legendary running back Walter Payton on November 1, 1999 as he lost his battle with a rare liver disease. The Bears named their indoor practice facility the "Walter Payton Center" in his honor the follow spring.

Printed in the United States
44257LVS00004B/1-3

9 781413 711073